BROKEN BEAUTY

A MAFIA ROMANCE

STELLA ANDREWS

Copyrighted Material
Copyright © Stella Andrews 2020
Stella Andrews has asserted her rights under the Copyright, Designs and Patents Act 1988 to be identified as the Author of this work.
This book is a work of fiction and except in the case of historical fact, any resemblance to actual persons, living or dead, is purely coincidental.

All rights reserved. No part of this book may be reproduced or transmitted in any form without written permission of the author, except by a reviewer who may quote brief passages for review purposes only.

18+ This book is for Adults only. If you are easily shocked and not a fan of sexual content then move away now.

NEWSLETTER SIGN UP

Sign up to my newsletter and download a free book

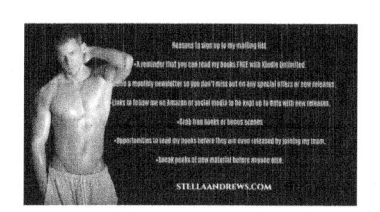

stellaandrews.com

BROKEN BEAUTY

"I ran from the beast into the arms of the Devil."

Sophia Moretti

Maverick
It takes a special kind of glue to mend a broken Angel.
She came to the right place—or so she thought.
Broken, traumatized and scared.
Her past was a place that had no business in her future.
But she ran to me.
She should have kept running.

Sophia
A man that keeps his secrets hidden behind eyes that are shielded by the blackest shade.

A prince shrouded in the helm of darkness to disguise a heart that is cloaked with the souls of the damned.

A wild Boar dressed in biker leathers, sunglasses and a stinking attitude.

A man who could pick a fight in an empty room.

A God of war.

Just the man I need right now.

As it turns out - I should have kept on running.

PROLOGUE

SOPHIA

I can hardly breathe. My chest hurts so much it's difficult to take in air. The sweat mingles with the terror as I urge my limbs to cooperate. The fear overtakes my reasoning because I thought I was safe. I *should* be safe, but the fact that someone's chasing me tells me otherwise.

As I crash through the trees, I struggle to see the danger in front of me. As my foot catches a tree root, it twists from under me and causes a sharp pain to cut through my body like a knife. I can feel them gaining on me, but I will not give up. I need to reach safety; I should never have believed I was safe here.

I am such a fool. I thought I could hide, but the fear that surrounds me like a vise tells me otherwise. I will never be free of it all the time the nightmares crowd my mind. I just wanted time to deal with it but it appears my time has run out.

I can hear him now. Gaining on me so fast I know I don't stand a chance. It's the acceptance of my fate that makes me stop and take a deep breath. Maybe it's time to turn and face my fear head on and deal with it the only way I know how because I'm tired of running. Tired of being scared and tired of life. If he has come for me, I would welcome the darkness. Just to close my eyes and never wake up is looking mighty attractive right now, so I stand my ground and turn and face whatever's behind me because it's what's in front of me I should be afraid of and nothing can be worse than that.

I almost dare not look, but as I raise my eyes, I swallow hard. I think it's a man stands a short distance away looking at me warily. I've never seen the like of him before and I stare in wonder at a beast that makes all other men look like kids. Wild dark hair touches his shoulders and his bare chest eclipses the sun. My heart flutters as I see the tattoo covering his biceps because that tells me he has every right to be here.

"You're on private property, darlin'."

His voice growls as he states a simple fact I know only too well. It was why I sought them out, a place that everyone fears which keeps the rest of the world outside.

So, I face him with indifference.

"I know."

He moves slowly forward and my heart beats faster as a strange excitement grips me. What will he do?

As he draws near, I see the sweat glistening on his tight abs and a smattering of dark hair that calls to the woman in me. He is magnificent and a world away from the men I usually keep the company of. Rough, feral and rugged - a real man. Not the suited and booted smooth criminals that usually occupy my world. This man is pure danger and yet as he moves closer and stares deep into my eyes, I step back in shock. *I know those eyes.*

He leans forward and his breath flutters across my face like a cooling breeze, fanning the flames of an interest that has no right being there. The dark eyes of the blackest shade penetrate my soul and makes my heart bleed because I know this man. There is no life in those eyes, just the tortured souls of the damned. An empty wretched soul that lost the ability to live and just exists in a tainted world of pain. *A killer's eyes.*

I know those eyes because I see them in the mirror every day. We are the same - we are lost.

"Then why are you here?"

His voice is husky and with deep tones that take no shit, so I shrug. "I live here."

Without warning and with a flick of his wrist, he grabs me hard and spins me against the trunk of a tree and contains me in a prison of muscle that has no key. He is so close our sweat joins and trickles like a river of lust to the ground and I feel his mouth inches from mine causing my mind to scramble.

"Since when?"

My first instinct is to try to struggle and free myself from his iron grip, but I feel strangely safe here. He keeps the whole world out and provides an impenetrable bubble that I could sure use right now. I am almost tempted to sag against him and cling on for grim death because I need that more than life itself at the moment but instead, I stare at him with a hard expression and say, "Since a month ago. I work for Ryder and Ashton; I help out with the kids."

At the mention of the man who rules this place with an iron fist should make him drop me like a hot coal, instead he leans even closer and growls, "Why should I believe you?"

"Because it's the truth. Now, if you don't mind, I would like to finish my run and grab a shower because I'm expected in just thirty minutes to help Ashton out with the kids."

He steps back and takes a long, lingering look, causing the blood to rush to every part of me that has a nerve ending. His hand holds me in position as he takes his time and I snap, "What's the matter, haven't you seen a woman before?"

He smirks and I watch with interest as his eyes flash and I

hold my breath. As moments go, this is the most interesting one of my life because I have never been treated like this before. The most interesting thing of all is that I am loving every minute of it and so, it's with the icy bucket of disappointment that he releases me and says gruffly, "Then you won't mind if I accompany you back. Call it your own personal protection."

As he steps away, I long to pull him back and use him as a safety shield. Suddenly, the space between us is suffocating me because it proves that once again, I'm on my own. He doesn't need to know that, so I shrug and start walking. "Suit yourself."

I start to jog and try to focus on anything but him. He settles in behind me and the only sound we can hear is of the twigs cracking under our feet as we head for home.

The Rubicon.

Home of the Twisted Reaper MC.

A band of bikers who clean up the government's pile of trash. Paid assassins who hide behind leather and steel and keep the world at arm's length. Men that fight wars every day of the week as they struggle to keep the filth from the streets of America. I owe them my life because these men saved me from a certain painful death when they rescued me from the building where I was held captive and facing a painful end.

They brought me here to return home with my brother, but that was never an option. Nobody knows what I went through during the darkest days of my life and the secret I learned. The only solution was to hide and hope it goes away because the reality is not worth thinking about. I walked away from my family to hide in a place where tortured souls go to heal and up until now, I have kept away from everyone but the kids and the women. I'm not interested in the men; they scare the hell out of me and *he* is no exception.

We don't speak all the way back. I try to empty my mind

and forget he's here because I need to pretend this is normal. I must build a new life for myself and this is the beginning of that process. There is no room for passengers on my journey, so my years of practice count as I slowly retreat into a shell I never really come out of.

CHAPTER 1

MAVERICK

I've obviously been away too long. As I stare with a hunger at the sweet ass clad in lycra bouncing before my eyes, I make a fist. Fuck me, this woman's impressive. It's unusual finding anyone at this time of the day, let alone running through the forest that surrounds the compound. It's why I thought she must be lost, but those green eyes that stared into mine had no fear in them, just a cold, dismissive superiority that instantly got my back up. It's why I behaved like a prick and held her against that tree. The beast inside me roared as she dared look at me with contempt. An ice queen, a frozen fucking princess that I am so done with right now. Hell, for the past five weeks I've been guarding one on the instructions of her fuck-head politician of a father.

The past few weeks have severely tested my patience as she did just about everything to stop me doing my job and I am so done with the lot of them. However, unlike the girl I just babysat, this one is all woman and the man inside me appreciates every fine curve of a body that's been created to ruin men everywhere. I loved the way her chest heaved and her breath hitched as she trembled against me. The cool edge to her eyes intrigued me and her blank expression told me more than she realized. I wonder why she's here?

Thinking about the past month makes me feel frustrated all over again. Ryder sent me to protect a politician's daughter who was receiving death threats in the mail. I followed her around and chased up every lead until I found the people responsible. Kids, stupid fucking kids who thought they could get away with blackmail and take the easy road in life. Students at the university she went to and no match for me. Well, they are now facing jail and I'm off the hook. I arrived home late last night and crawled to my pit, glad to be home. The early morning run is my usual stress reliever, followed by a warm, willing whore to settle the beast inside me. However, this woman is no whore, unlike the ones who sleep within our steel-clad walls. I could tell that the moment I saw those cold eyes staring at me with no spark of interest. Who is she? I feel as if I know her; somehow, she is familiar to me. A nanny, she says, not fucking likely.

We jog into the yard and she places her hands on her knees and gasps for breath, giving me an impressive view to feast my eyes on. As she straightens up, she shakes her head. "Don't you have clothes?"

Looking down at my bare chest and shorts, I shrug. "Listen, darlin', I do my own laundry and because I hate it more than anything, I try not to add to the pile. Why, what's it to you, anyway?"

"Nothing. If you ran naked, it wouldn't affect me; I just wondered, that's all."

I take a moment to picture what she would look like running bare chested through the forest and grin. "You should try it sometime, it's quite liberating."

"In your dreams because that's the only place you'll ever see my naked body."

Spinning on her heels, she walks away toward the rear of the compound and I follow her with interest, making her turn and snap, "You don't have to follow me you know. I can find my own room without a guide."

"Who said I was following you? I live here too, remember?"

She turns and marches quickly away and I follow, once again appreciating the fine view of her ass until she says over her shoulder, "Stop staring at my ass."

I say nothing and carry on following until we reach the block where the whores have their rooms and then watch as she punches the code in the door and disappears through it without looking back. Just before it closes Millie heads out and squeals as she sees me. "Maverick, when did you get back?"

She jumps into my arms and as my arms fold around her, she wraps her legs around me and whispers, "I've missed you."

Great, just what I need. Millie has made no secret of her liking for me and yet all I've ever done is have sex with her. I've never promised her anything but the usual agreement between the Reapers and the many girls who live here, with no strings attached and no commitment needed. Just two people taking comfort from each other when the need arises. So, I set her down gently and say coolly. "Good to see you, darlin'."

Her face falls as she senses the barriers shutting her out and shrugs. "It's good to see you, honey. Will you be in the bar later?"

"Not sure."

Once again, her face falls making me feel like a complete bastard, but it's how it must be. I'm not here to find love. I'm here to shut it out, and so I nod toward the door. "Who was that, I found her jogging in the woods?"

"Who, Sophia?"

"Yes, what's her story?"

"She's been here about a month, not long after you left. The Reapers rescued her from some guy who had her chained to a wall and beat the shit out of her. She won't talk though. She stays in her room and just runs in her spare time. When she's not running, she looks after the kids. They're the only ones who drag a smile out of her because aside from them, she's interested in no one."

"Why was she held captive?"

"I don't know, maybe you should ask her if you want answers?"

Millie snaps irritably which isn't like her and then says coolly, "Anyway, I'm off to re-stock the bar. Good to see you back, Mav, maybe look me up later if you need company."

She flounces off and I groan inside. Now I've upset her. She didn't like me asking questions about Sophia, that was obvious. Maybe I should keep away from the bar because Millie is starting to overstep the mark. I don't want to give her false hope because I'm not interested. I thought she knew that—apparently not.

CHAPTER 2

SOPHIA

I may have left him at the door, but he follows me inside. I can't shake the image of the infuriating man who held me captive for a brief second in the woods. He followed me back, but even through the silence we communicated. I know he stared at my ass the whole way back, it's as if I *feel* him. Every part of me understands that man and the way his mind works. It's as if we are cut from the same cloth and unlike the other men who live here, I don't want to keep my distance from him.

When I looked back, it was to see one of the women held against him and for some strange reason I was jealous. That alone makes me mad because I have no right to be jealous of anyone. I made my choice and now it's up to me to deal with it. The trouble is, I don't know how and so with a sigh; I head to the shower and get ready for the only part of my day that counts.

Exactly thirty minutes later, I find my way out back to the home of the president who runs this MC club. Ryder King. Hard-assed bastard, but the kindest man I think I've ever met. Along with his wife, they took me in and didn't press for details. They gave me a job helping care for the kids around here because that's where I feel happiest. I have never been around children. There were none when I was growing up and when I lived with my brother, it was just the two of us along with the guards. To say I've lived a sheltered life is an understatement, but what happened when I was taken will haunt me to my dying day.

Shutting the memories down before they destroy me again, I knock on the door and wait for Ashton to let me in. I'm here to entertain Cassie, her adorable daughter because Ashton has her hands full with the latest addition to their family. Three weeks ago, Ashton gave birth to the most beautiful baby boy. Just like his father, Caspian King is sure to be a heartbreaker. Beautiful blue eyes sparkle beneath a crop of dark wild curls and he holds a woman's heart the minute she looks at him. I am no exception because that little angel is the light of my own dark life. It's the eyes of the innocent who look at me with so much trust that fills my heart with hope.

Can I love? I never have before but there is something about the children that surround me that stir black into white. I find myself craving their company and hearing their laughter. It soothes my weary soul and if I stay here forever with them, I would die happy.

The door opens and I take a step back as the man of the house fills the opening.

Ryder King is the sort of man that steals the breath from inside you and replaces it with electricity. Impressive in every way from his startling good looks to his rock-hard abs. He wears the badge of authority as if it was born part of him and I know there is not a man, woman or child here who doesn't love and respect every inch of him.

He looks at me with interest and nods. "Morning, darlin', anything to report?"

I smile because he says this every day. They are patient with me because from the moment I stepped foot inside their home, I have kept for my reasons for doing so to myself. At first, I wouldn't even speak but gradually they have eased my mind and allowed me to breathe again but I'm not ready to tell them why I won't return home—not yet, maybe not ever.

So, I shake my head and stare at him with my usual blank look. "No."

Nodding, he steps aside. "Then I'll let you get on with your day."

He moves away and I smile to myself. The same conversation every day for three weeks. I wonder when I'll be able to let my guard down and trust them with the full horror story that is mine to write the ending of.

"Morning, Pia."

A scream alerts me to business and I laugh as Ryder's daughter Cassie races toward me like a tornado and jumps into my arms. "Morning, Angel, have you been good for your mama?"

I hear laughter and see Ashton watching us from the doorway with Caspian in her arms, gazing at Cassie fondly. "She's always good, aren't you, honey?"

Ashton rolls her eyes as Cassie says solemnly, "Yes, mommy."

We share a grin because like her father, Cassie is a handful that is only encouraged by him. Not afraid to stand her ground and batter a bully to the ground, Ashton is forever being called into the principal's office to 'discuss' her behavior. Along with Jack, Brewer and Lou's son, they make a formidable team and need a firm hand.

Ashton smiles, which draws an immediate response from me. A beautiful woman who is the antithesis of everyone else in this house. Beautiful blonde hair and blue eyes, with a southern drawl that instantly makes you feel at home. The light to Ryder's shade and the best mother these kids could ever wish for. She has her own demons that vanished the moment she claimed Ryder's heart and they share a love so pure; it makes me believe in happy ever afters.

"Come in, honey. Cassie wants to do some coloring, while she fetches it, I'll make you a coffee."

"I should be making the coffee; you have your hands full."

Looking down, Ashton smiles softly at the gorgeous boy in her arms and then holds him out to me. "Maybe you could mind him while I make them."

I need no further invitation and take him from her with an eagerness that surprises even me. It feels so natural to hold the precious bundle in my arms and I breathe deeply and fill my lungs with his heavenly scent. Pure innocence is the sweetest balm to a wounded soul.

As he stares up at me with those gorgeous eyes, I feel an emotion that has escaped me all my life - love.

"How was your run?"

Ashton calls across from the kitchen and I make my way inside and take a seat at the breakfast bar, holding her Prince Caspian in my arms.

"Different."

"In what way?"

"I wasn't alone."

She turns and raises her eyes and I can't help but feel the flush creep across my skin as she says, "Who was there?"

"I'm not sure of his name, one of the guys."

"What did he look like?"

If Ashton can sense any difference in me, she is keeping it well hidden, so I shrug and say coolly, "Bit of a beast if I'm honest. Longish dark hair and a complete brute of a man. No manners and no clothes, actually."

Her eyes widen as she laughs softly, "Not always a bad thing."

"Hmm, maybe. He was running in just a very tiny pair of shorts."

We share a grin and then she says carefully, "What happened?"

I miss out the physical contact part and shrug. "He escorted me back. I think he thought I was an intruder."

"Must have been Maverick then."

I stare at her in surprise and she laughs. "He's the only one who doesn't know you're here. He's been away for a month and must have arrived back late last night. He's also the only one who runs around here so early in the morning and hardly ever wears a top."

"Yes, he said he does his own laundry."

"He spoke to you?" Ashton looks surprised.

"Why? Doesn't he normally?"

"Not really. He's the strong, silent type. He talks to the guys, but the girls get nothing from him. Other than the obvious, I mean."

She giggles and I feel a flash of jealousy that surprises me as I think of him with the girls that live here. Remembering the one from earlier, it leaves a bitter taste in my mouth and as Caspian starts to cry, it breaks up the conversation and Ashton says apologetically, "I should go and feed him. He's a bit overdue because Ryder was late leaving."

She blushes a little and I can only imagine what pleasure that man brings to her life as she gets a faraway look in her eye. She smiles softly. "Anyway, I shouldn't be long. If Cassie loses interest, I think Jack is around today and Lou said you could visit anytime. I've got the nurse coming, so will tied up for a bit. Help yourself to anything you need and call if you need me."

I watch as she takes her baby and envy her the life she has. A loving husband and a beautiful family with the most amazing home, surrounded by the most loyal of friends. This place is hell on earth to outsiders but Utopia to the occupants that live within its steel walls.

As I wait, I think about the man I met in the woods. Maverick. A free spirit. It suits him.

I wonder if I'll ever see him again because I like to keep away from the men. I'm not interested in becoming another one of their booty calls and to be honest, they scare the hell out of me, anyway.

When I lived with the guards, they respected who I was and my position. I have only ever been with one man and that was a mistake of the worst kind. I have no interest in repeating that mistake, so keep hidden in my ivory tower. But Maverick, there was something different about him, yet familiar at the same time. Who is he?

CHAPTER 3

MAVERICK

Now I'm back and ready to catch up. Once I've showered and changed, I head to the kitchen to grab some breakfast. I share my space with the single guys among us. We keep our own place clean and do our own chores, which includes cooking, so I set to work as I've always done, keeping everything clean and in the military fashion we're accustomed to. By the time I've sat down to attack my food, one of the other guys heads my way and sets about doing the same thing. "Hey, Maverick, I heard you were back."

"Hey, Rebel, how are things?"

"Usual. You haven't missed much. I heard you had a particularly difficult mission."

He laughs as I growl. "Fucking spoiled kid. Ryder owes me big time for that one."

"Maybe you could take some time off. Go on a road trip?"

Sometimes the guys like to take off after an individual mission, but I'm not one of them. I live to work and work to live and have no interest in my own company for weeks on end.

"No, I'm good."

"I'm guessin' you need a little female company to set you back on track, it must have been hard dealing with shit yourself for a whole month."

Pushing my plate back, I'm surprised to find that's the last thing on my mind as an image of the new woman comes to me.

"Maybe."

"Maybe? What's happened to you, man? I thought you'd be balls deep in one of the whores five seconds after you arrived. I'm sure Millie would oblige."

He laughs and I shake my head. "Not interested. She's making noises that I don't wanna hear."

Grabbing the chair beside me, Rebel looks interested. "She catchin' feelings?"

"Maybe but just in case, I'm keeping my distance."

He nods because like me, Rebel isn't interested in grabbing an old lady anytime soon and I know he understands.

Then he whistles. "We got a new broken angel to mend when you left."

My ears prick up immediately, but I say nothing.

"Stays in her room every night and keeps hidden in the day."

"What's her story?"

Suddenly, Rebel looks nervous which isn't like him—at all and my nerves stand to attention.

"Listen, man, I'm sorry to be the bearer of bad news but she's the sister of some mafia don."

I make a fist under the table but set my features in stone and wait for him to finish.

"She was kidnapped by some guy out for revenge and nearly didn't make it. We stormed the building and got her out, along with another woman and two kids. They were all in a bad way, which is nothing to what the guy who took them was like when we finished with him."

I almost can't speak and growl, "Why is she still here?"

"Don't know. Word is, she won't go back to her brother. Won't speak and won't leave. He left the same night and took the guy who kidnapped her with him. Not sure what happened after that, but we've been warned off. She's being left to heal and when she's ready, she'll talk to Ryder. Sorry man, I know you don't do mafia but you were bound to find out."

"It's fine. I'm glad you told me."

Pushing back my plate, I've suddenly lost my appetite. Mafia. My blood runs cold at the mere mention of the word.

Now I know who she is.

∼

IT DOESN'T TAKE me long to find my way to Ryder's door. He wanted a debrief and after I tell him the details, he sits back and nods with approval. "Good job, Maverick, I know it was a hard one."

"You could say that."

The door opens and Ryder's right-hand man, Snake, heads into the office and nods. "Hey, Mav, good to see you."

I nod as he takes the seat beside me and groans. "I wish Bonnie would hurry up and get back from her mom's, I'm all over the place."

Ryder grins. "She's only been gone two days, what's the matter, you going soft?"

Snake grins wickedly. "As it happens, quite the opposite. It's ok for guys like Maverick who can crook their little finger at any available woman in the bar and be balls deep inside ten minutes but I don't have that luxury."

Ryder rolls his eyes as I grin because from the looks of

Snake you wouldn't think he would be told to do anything and especially by a slip of a girl like Bonnie. However, we all know who holds the true power in their relationship as Snake groans and rubs his crotch.

Ryder rolls his eyes. "That's disgusting, take it to the shower."

Snake grins. "Who says I haven't already? What can I say, I'm insatiable?"

Shaking his head, Ryder turns to me and I watch his expression change and prepare for what I know is coming.

"I have another job for you."

"No."

He raises his eyes and the atmosphere changes in the room. Gone is the easy banter and in its place is an edgy tension that causes Snake to lean forward and Ryder's eyes to narrow as he says gruffly, "Explain."

"You're gonna ask me to take on the new girl."

"And why is that a problem?"

I make a fist which is the only indication that I'm on the edge and you could hear a pin drop in the room as my two superiors look at me with a challenge in their eyes.

Nobody disobeys orders here—ever. But like my name suggests, I don't always follow the rule book, so I say with a hard edge to my voice. "I don't do mafia, you know that."

I know there is nothing they can say to that because I made it perfectly clear the minute I arrived. It's my one rule that I will not break and Ryder knows it because he nods respectfully and leans back. "Then we have a problem."

Snake also leans back and I can breathe again. The last thing I want is to antagonize the two hardest men I will ever meet, but I have my rules and this is precisely the reason why.

Ryder turns to Snake. "Has Bonnie had any luck?"

"No. She won't open up. God only knows what that fuck-head did to her, but she's shut down completely. You can tell that by the look in her eyes."

I hold my breath because I know that look. I've lived with it my entire life and yet I have no compassion for the alluring mafia princess because this is one shit storm I'm shielding myself from.

Ryder just sighs and says with resignation. "Then we give her more time."

He stands and nods toward the door.

"Come on, I need a beer. When it involves women, I know shit, anyway."

I follow them out, but a beer is the furthest thing from my mind. I need to get out of this place before I do something I'll regret.

CHAPTER 4

SOPHIA

Cassie runs ahead and I struggle to keep up with her. We decided to take Lou up on her offer because Ashton looked as if she could use the rest once Caspian was settled.

We are heading toward their pretty house nearby and Cassie is excited to spend time with her best friend.

I laugh as she yells for him at the top of her voice and it's not long before the door slams open and he races out, catching her hand and dragging her inside.

Lou follows him out and laughs. "They'll never change. Like two peas in a pod."

I nod in agreement and I can feel her staring at me with a thoughtful expression and wonder what's running through her mind. I know they're curious. They don't ask but they obviously have questions they know I don't want to answer and they're right.

She smiles and says slowly. "You know, honey, I promised Jack a treat today if he completed his chores but I'm needed to help out in the office. I don't suppose you could take them into town for an ice-cream; it would really help out?"

I stare at her in horror as the panic sets in and I say in a shaky voice, "No. I can't. I'm so sorry, Lou, I'll mind them here but please don't ask me to take them off site."

"Why not, honey, is something troubling you?"

Now I know why Lou is considered a wiley woman and know this was a test to get me to open up, so I backtrack and shrug. "No, I just don't feel confident taking the two of them out on my own. If anything happened to them, I would never forgive myself."

I almost can't get the words out because they remind me of a different situation with two other children and I almost can't breathe as I battle the panic attack that memory brings on.

"Hey, Maverick."

My heart lurches as Lou looks behind me and I feel myself instantly tense as I hear his husky voice, "What's up, Lou?"

I almost see a wicked glint enter her eyes as she smiles. "Can I ask a favor?"

"Anything for you."

I think I hold my breath as she says sweetly, "I've asked Sophia to take the kids to town for an ice-cream but she's not confident on her own. Would you go with them?"

I daren't look because this is turning out even worse than expected and from the narrowing of Lou's eyes, I can tell he is none too happy at being asked. The silence is a little awkward until Jack and Cassie come racing out and Cassie shouts, "Maverick," before leaping into his arms. Jack does the same and his laughter shocks me into turning around and stare in disbelief as he holds them each under one arm as they scream with pleasure.

Cassie shouts, "Please come, Maverick, say you will, pleeeez!"

Jack nods vigorously and Maverick shakes his head. "Of

course, I will, only if you're good soldiers though, there will be no messing around on my watch."

They nod with a solemn promise that causes Lou to roll her eyes and I grin.

Then Maverick looks at me and I feel my heart flutter for a different reason. It's all there in that one look. Hostility, danger and a promise of something that will be out of control unless we keep a tight lid on it. Those eyes are not the sort you want directed on you because they promise the most devastating storm ahead and I shake inside.

He nods respectfully. "Are you ready, darlin'?"

I look at Lou with a mixture of desperation and fear and she smiles encouragingly. "Go with him, Sophia. You need to get away from here to a touch of normal. It's not good for you to be sheltered from the outside world and the longer you leave it, the harder it will be."

I feel so torn and totally out of my depth and Lou draws close and whispers, "Go with Maverick, honey. He won't let anything happen to any of you. You're safe with him."

As I look at the man himself, I beg to disagree. I am not safe from him, it's all there in his eyes as he dares me to back out now. Maybe it's just a little of the old fire in me that sparks because I find myself nodding and saying with a braver voice than I feel, "Fine, if you insist."

She smiles with encouragement before heading back inside and Maverick says gruffly, "Follow me."

He turns and strides off with his two passengers wriggling under his arms and I follow with a resignation that has been thrust upon me.

~

IT DOESN'T TAKE LONG for us to reach a large SUV in the yard and as the kids scoot into the back, I almost feel a panic attack coming on. I can't do this. I can't go there—the outside world. Bad things happen there and I'm not ready.

I must be frozen to the spot before I feel a rough hand fold around mine and a soft husky voice say in a whisper, "I've got you, darlin', you're safe with me."

I raise my eyes to his and beg to disagree. His words may say one thing, but the eyes say another. However, his touch is like an electric shock re-starting my frozen limbs to life and I feel my legs move as if I'm a puppet controlled by him as I allow him to help me into the passenger seat beside him.

Trying so hard to get my breathing under control, I stare at the ground and count to ten. I'll be ok, I can do this. It's just ice-cream.

"Pia, what's your favorite flavor?"

Cassie's voice brings me back and I say softly, "Vanilla."

Maverick snorts beside me and whispers, "That figures."

For a moment, I just stare at him in confusion and then the penny drops and I feel myself blushing furiously as the look he sends me tells me vanilla would definitely not be included on his menu.

As he starts the car, Cassie and Jack start chattering excitedly in the back and I lean back and close my eyes, letting their soft, innocent voices wash my fears away. I'll be ok, I *must* be ok because being *not* ok, is no longer an option.

CHAPTER 5

MAVERICK

How the fuck did this happen? I left Ryder and Snake, intent on burning rubber, not taking two kids and the one woman I should avoid most in the world on a trip into town. Lou had me over a barrel and she knew it. How could I say no to her, or the children? I should have done. I should have just walked away, but one look at Sophia and the terror in her eyes made up my mind in an instant. She's petrified and it can only be because of that bastard that took her. The trouble is, I don't want to know the details. I don't want to hear her story and I don't want to spend any time with her because if I do, I may have to act and I am not prepared to destroy everything I've worked so hard to build the past few years, to be destroyed in a heartbeat.

Yes, this woman will destroy me and everything I've worked hard for if I let her and so I must keep away for both our sakes.

I let the kids chatter the nonsense that is usual for their age and try to distance my mind from the woman sitting like a statue beside me. I may not see her but I feel her and it's surprising me more than I thought. I can't tear my mind away from the scent of the woman sitting beside me and find myself imagining inhaling every part of her as I make her mine. I want to growl in frustration because she doesn't know it but she *is* mine. She always was and now fucked up fate has delivered her to me on a platter. But I'm not hungry and I should hold that thought because the beast in me is roaring to be set free. Just a fraction of movement causes my attention to stand guard and the air cracks between us with an electricity that could set us on fire.

By the time we reach town we have not shared two words and that's how it's gonna stay if I get my way. The kids will distract us and then I will return them home and get the hell out of here. Maybe a road trip is just what I need right now because I need to get my shit together.

Fucking mafia, how ironic is that?

We find a space outside for the truck and by the time we head inside, I've got my head in the game.

Grabbing a booth in the corner, I curse as the kids slide in beside each other, leaving me to share the confined space with Sophia.

She edges into the corner and looks around her fearfully, shrinking into her seat so as not to draw attention to herself. The waitress heads over and looks at us with interest. "What can I get you all?"

"Strawberry please."

Cassie smiles with an excitement which makes me chuckle inside. So happy over an ice-cream, kids are easily pleased.

"Chocolate for me please?"

Jack grins and I have to smile because he is one heap of trouble waiting to grow up into an even greater one. In fact, they both are because these kids don't know it yet but they will have the world at their feet and god help anyone who gets in their way.

I turn to Sophia and she smiles nervously. "Um…"

I quickly interrupt, "She'll have the house special with lots of toppings, same for me."

Sophia opens her mouth to speak and I whisper, "Allow me to introduce you to the wild side."

I wink as she stares at me in shock and I laugh softly, whispering, "Vanilla is most definitely off the menu for you darlin'. Trust me, you'll love every mouthful."

I love the flush that creeps across her face and the spark that ignites those gorgeous green eyes. She runs her tongue around her lips and I inch a little closer, wanting nothing more than to lick the ice-cream off her naked body and hear her moan my name. I don't think either of us remember there are kids present because her breath hitches and she breathes a little faster and then blushes as Cassie says in a sing song voice, "Sophia and Maverick sitting in a tree, k.i.s.s.i.n.g."

Jack laughs loudly and Sophia looks at them in shock as I grin. Fucking kids.

Shaking her head, Sophia says quickly, "Honestly, Cassie, you've got that wrong."

Cassie grins at me and I wink, making her giggle and whisper behind her hand to Jack, who nods vigorously. Hell, even these kids see it and so I try to distract my attention onto them.

"So, you've got a new baby brother since I was gone, what's he like?"

"Daddy said he's named after a prince because his daddy's a King."

Cassie looks so proud it draws a rare smile from my lips and Jack looks a little put out. "I heard he cries all the time."

"He does, but that's what babies do; mommy told me."

Cassie looks so serious as Jack shrugs. "Babies can't play football or climb trees. I'm glad he's not in our house."

"Shut up, Jack, don't talk bad about my brother or I'll punch you."

Cassie looks so fierce I almost want to laugh out loud and thankfully the ice-creams arrive in the nick of time, diverting their attention from a possible fist fight.

The kids fall on their ice-creams as if they've never seen one before, and Sophia looks at hers warily as it stands before her in all its decadent glory.

I take my spoon and god only knows why, I push it in the middle of the bowl and offer a huge spoonful to the woman looking wary beside me.

"Open."

Without saying another word, I hold the spoon against her lips and Cassie says loudly, "Try it, Pia, it's the best."

Slowly and tentatively she opens her mouth and as I push the spoon inside, I imagine a very different part of me in its place. As her lips close around the metal shaft and pull the cream inside, I discover a raging hard on that's no business being there.

I watch intently for a reaction and she half closes her eyes and moans with approval and then opens her eyes and stares at me with those sparkling green eyes and nods. "You were right, it is good."

For a moment, I can't form words, but then I'm aware of the amused expressions on the kids' faces and pull the spoon away quickly and turn my attention to the ice-cream instead. "Told you, I'm guessing vanilla is off the menu in the future."

"Maybe, but then again, I've never been a fan of ice-cream."

She says it slowly and with a sadness to her voice that causes me to look and I see the loneliness in her eyes that only one who knows what that feels like can truly understand. She bows her head with a sigh and continues to play with her food as the kids chatter about school and some kid called Billy Merino.

I tune out and lower my voice, whispering, "You can shut the world away, darlin', or you can open the door and let it in. You might find it's not as scary as you think it is."

I feel her tense and she looks down and I watch the shutters slam shut as she says tightly, "Who said I wanted to? Maybe I prefer my own company."

"If you do, it's because you haven't found the right company to keep."

Leaning back, she half turns and directs those cold eyes at me and sneers. "And you think that's you?"

"I'm not saying that. Have I asked to be here? No, the reason I'm asking is that I can tell you're in a bad place right now and probably don't know where the exit is. I've been there and can show the way. Not because I have any other motive than helping a fellow human being in trouble. It's what we do. We build up broken angels and mend their wings so they can fly again. If you won't listen to me, there are fifty more where we come from who would only be too happy to show you the right path. Think about it."

I turn away and carry on eating and say nothing more. All the time I want to punch my fist through the table because how those words left my lips, god only knows. I'm not interested in anything about her, but my stupid mouth has other ideas. Do I want to help this woman, fuck no because in helping her, I'm sending myself straight back to hell?

CHAPTER 6

SOPHIA

I'm struggling to breathe. Just being here is enough to break me, but sitting beside Maverick is a whole new experience. Fear is something I've lived with my whole life. From an early age I was guarded and told to trust no one because absolutely everybody was out to get me. I was born with a target on my back and it was only a matter of time before it got hit. Well, I was hit bad and for the past five years I have allowed myself to be controlled by my family—the one remaining member of it at least. When I was taken, I was told something that shows I should keep on running because I will never be safe. It's why I want to hide away from the world in a place I know they can't find me.

But now, sitting here doing something most normal people take for granted, is proving to me how different I really am. I feel as if I'm having an out-of-body experience and yet sitting beside Maverick calms me. He keeps the world away because for some reason I feel safe with him. He is unconventional and a world away from the usual men I have lived with all my life. Yet there is something so fearless about him that builds up my confidence like it never has before. He is cold, calculating and so incredibly hot, I can't see straight when he's around. What would it feel like to be with a man like him—with any man because the one experience I had sworn me off men for life? Yet when he looks at me with those wicked eyes, he strips me bare inside. He causes my blood to boil and my inhibitions to melt because I want to sample what it would feel like having a man like him show me what I've been missing.

So, I sit in silence trying hard to gather my frantic thoughts around me and then he says loudly, "Come, let's get you all home before they send out the search party."

Cassie and Jack look disappointed. "Please can we stay a little longer?" Jack frowns and Maverick says in his husky, deep voice, "You got a good reason to stay soldier?"

Jack looks him in the eye and sits up tall and straight. "My mom told me I had to learn my spellings before dinner, sir and I want her to forget about it."

I stifle a grin as Maverick turns to Cassie. "And you?"

She does the same and says loudly, "My mommy told me I had to tidy my room and I want to watch Cinderella."

They look at Maverick with faces full of hope and he growls, "A good soldier keeps a clean house and keeps up with his studies. Permission to stay denied."

The kids look crushed and Maverick fixes them with a stern look. "If you're good and do as you're told, I will bring you both back here for ice-cream next week. Deal?"

Their screams cause a few heads to turn in our direction, making me shrink even further down in my seat.

Without warning, a hand shoots out and takes mine firmly and Maverick growls, "I've got you, darlin', nothing can get through me to you."

Resisting the urge to snatch my hand away, I find instead my hand clasping his so tightly it must hurt. Physical contact alone is a strange experience for me because none of the guards would dare touch me and my brother certainly never showed me any affection this way. It takes my breath away as I realize how nice it is.

As we walk to the front of the diner, I feel the stares of the people all around. They must think we're a family and it shocks me to realize I wish we were. Do I want this—a family of my own one day? Family means something very different to me and yet, here, with Maverick beside me and the two most adorable kids in tow, I find I want this more than any of the riches I've enjoyed until now. This is worth all the gold in the world - a real family.

Maverick settles the cheque and then takes my hand once again and almost pulls me from the diner. Cassie and Jack start play-fighting until Maverick growls at them to stop. Then he opens the door and barks at them to belt up and shut up and slams the door behind them.

Then he takes my hand once again but before opening the passenger door, leans in until my back is firm against the metal and he crowds the world out. Suddenly, it is only him. He is all around me and I see nothing but those dark, dead eyes looking at me as if I'm prey. Leaning in, he whispers huskily, "As soon as those kids are safely back with their mamas, you and me are gonna talk."

I stare at him in fear and his lips brush against my ear as he says firmly, "Non-negotiable. It's your choice, either you open up to me, or you live in fear your whole life. That life is found when you dance between your greatest desire and your biggest fear. We just need to discover what that desire is darlin' and use it to set you free."

The fact he is so close makes me lose my mind. I can feel the heat from his skin in the air that I breathe and it is laced with a yearning for something he can offer me that I sorely need right now—hope. Yes, Maverick is asking to help me and I would be a fool to turn him away. However, those eyes tell a different story and both of us know that in opening myself up to him, will bring with it a different set of problems altogether. Will I step into the pit of hell and make a deal with the devil? It certainly feels that way because at this moment I would do anything for this man because for the first time in my life—I am interested.

∼

BY THE TIME we reach the Rubicon, I finally know why it bears that name. The point of no return—it certainly feels that way.

As we pull up in the yard, I see Ryder standing with a few of the others and watch as Cassie shrieks and runs to him, jumping straight into his arms. The look on his face brings a lump to my throat as he holds her close and strokes her hair lovingly, whispering in her ear something that makes her giggle. How I wish my own father was a man like that. The tears burn as I think about my own family and as I brush them away, Maverick growls. "Stay with me darlin'."

We walk across and I don't miss the interest in Ryder's eyes as he sees who I'm with and then he smirks, prompting Maverick to snap, "You can thank Lou for this and just for the record, it's a favor, a one off that means shit."

Ryder laughs softly causing Maverick to mutter under his breath and before I know what's happening, he grabs my hand once again and pulls me after him at speed. I almost fall over my own feet as he drags me god only knows where and I don't miss the amusement on the men's faces as they watch us go.

Before long we reach the building where the Reapers have their rooms and my heart starts racing inside. Surely, we're not going there—to his room.

Apparently, we are because he doesn't even give me a

choice before punching in the entry code and slamming the door behind us.

"Slow down."

I plead with him as he drags me behind him and he growls, "Let's get this over with."

I feel hurt and just a little betrayed as I sense his anger and fight back the urge to tell him to go to hell, but something deep inside me wants this conversation. I want to open up to someone and see if he can make it all go away. It may as well be him because I don't care what he thinks of me - of my family but I do care what happens next because I know I can't carry on living like this.

By the time we reach his room, I've won my own argument with myself. If he wants me to open up, he had better be prepared for what he hears because it's not the happiest of tales and I expect he can do nothing about it, anyway. If anything, it might buy me a bit more time here under their protection because even I know I'm on borrowed time. They don't owe me anything and it's only a matter of time before they tire of me and send me right back to hell.

CHAPTER 7

MAVERICK

I'm not sure why I changed my mind, but it probably has something to do with the fact Sophia is obviously scared shitless. Despite who she is, I can't stand seeing a woman like that and I keep on telling myself I'll hear her out then offload the problem to Ryder to deal with. It's not gonna become mine because I don't do mafia, end of. However, even I know I'm fast falling into that world where the shadows claim your soul.

As we reach my room, I don't even try to be gentle and snap, "Sit."

Pointing to my couch, I almost push her down and she stares around her in amazement.

"You live here?"

She says it in shock and I snap, "What's the matter with it, not your usual standard, Princess?"

"No." She shakes her head and appears to forget why we're here because she says with surprising emotion, "I love it."

I look around in surprise because it's nothing special, but she shakes her head and whispers, "It's perfect. I never knew."

"Knew what?"

I am genuinely concerned about this woman's sanity because it's just a room, but she turns to me with tears in her eyes which makes me sit down hard beside her in shock. "It's just like home."

"That, I find very hard to believe, darlin'."

I'm no fool and my modern, loft style space, is nothing like a mafia mansion and she shakes her head. "I have my own suite of rooms and they are just like this. My brother has the usual finery associated with wealth but I like it simple, modern and tasteful. It's like being back at home without the fear of what that involves."

"You fear your home."

I stare at her in disbelief because I know how much of a fortress that must be. Her eyes fill with tears and she nods. "Yes." Her voice is but a whisper and her shoulders begin to shake as she returns to a dark place in her soul.

The words hang in the air we breathe because this is a turning point for her and I don't want to scare it away. Instead, I do something I never do and wrap my arms around her and pull her close, stroking her hair to comfort a woman who is probably not used to it. She shivers in my arms and I know she is battling hard, so I whisper, "Relax, nothing will hurt you here. We can stay here and just talk for as long as you need. I won't judge and I won't react. Tell me your fears, darlin' because the bravest person is the one who is scared the most. That bravery will win your battle for you."

She holds me tight and as her arms wrap around me, I feel something I should run away from as fast as possible because now she's in my arms, I never want her to leave.

Then she says in a whisper, "It's all my fault."

"What is?"

"I killed my parents."

I didn't expect to hear that but just hold her a little tighter and say softly, "Go on."

"I thought I was in love with a rival family's son. You know the sort of thing, Romeo and Juliet had nothing on us. The thing is, he used me to find out everything he could about my family. I swear I never knew, but he promised me he loved me."

She starts to sob and yet I say nothing. I will not let words snap her back from the past; she needs to get this out. So, I stroke her hair carefully and she says in a small voice, "We were going to run away. He told me we would get married and be together, away from the world we both lived in. Be a normal couple and find a place together and get married, have kids, you know the sort of thing most normal people take for granted. I fell for his words because I truly thought he meant them. It was exciting and I couldn't agree fast enough. That day we met and took a cab to a motel in the next town. We checked in under false names and it felt like we had broken out of prison and the dark clouds cleared. I was so in love with him and couldn't wait for our new life. We unpacked and Carlos wasted no time in taking something I was only too happy to give him."

She stops and cries a little harder and my heart freezes as the fury consumes my soul. "He was so cold and rough. I thought it would be magical and like the stories tell you. It was anything but and hurt like hell. If I felt anything, it was pain and he still didn't stop. He wouldn't stop, even when I cried and told him it hurt. He placed his hand over my mouth and told me it always did the first time and to shut up before someone called the cops. I never thought it would end and prayed it would be over soon because I have never felt such pain."

I almost wish I never asked because now I'm feral. Imagining what that fucking bastard did to this woman leaves a bitter taste for revenge in my mouth. Revenge I know has already been claimed by another and I can only hope it was a painful end for a man who makes Satan look like an angel.

She sobs hard against my chest and still I say nothing. Just stroke her hair, over and over again as I try to drive the image from my mind of a man who raped a girl while she begged him to stop.

"I didn't know it was wrong, Maverick. I thought it was like that for everyone. He finally stopped and just lit a cigarette and told me to go and get cleaned up because he couldn't bear the smell of me. Even then I didn't question him. There was so much blood everywhere and I felt sick. I still feel that cold water of a dirty shower that had probably never been cleaned, as I washed away my sin. The blood mingled with the dirt and made me feel ashamed. I still remember how empty I felt when I should have been so happy. I suppose I took too long because when I returned, he'd gone."

She slumps against me and starts to cry and I know it took a lot for her to get those words out. The feelings she has are ones she's had to live with all these years and yet it's as if they're still raw and never gone away. Time has not been a great healer in her case because this woman is as broken as they come. So, I do nothing but continue to hold her as she cries like a baby and as my arms tighten around her, I take her pain and make it my own.

She says no more and I don't press her. If anything, she's exhausted, so I pull back and wipe her tears away and say as softly as I can. "Listen, darlin', that took a lot of guts to share that with me and now you need to rest. Lie down on my couch and I'll find you a blanket. You can rest here while I fix us something to eat. I won't be long and nobody will disturb you here. Are you ok with that because I don't think you should be on your own right now?"

The gratitude in her eyes makes my heart break all over again as she nods shyly and lays her head on the cushion and closes her eyes. A lone tear falls as her lids close and my heart twists inside. She looks so fragile lying on my leather couch and as I reach for the blanket nearby, I am careful to tuck it around her without disturbing her. Just for a minute, I take a long look at the beauty sleeping so peacefully on my couch. It took all of a few seconds for her breathing to change and the tears are still damp on her cheeks as her face falls into a relaxed pose. Without the fear and anxiety pinching her features, this woman shines. She is majestic and yet has an innocence that is the opposite of who she should be. A polished, flawless diamond in a stinking pit and she shines despite the filth that surrounds her. Strangely, I feel my own tension leave me as I look at her lying there and feel an irresistible urge to lie right beside her and just marvel at what nature can create. Instead, I drag my sorry ass to the kitchen and do as I promised and make us some food to help get us through a long night ahead.

CHAPTER 8

SOPHIA

For the first time in more years than I can remember, I sleep with no nightmares to tear at my soul.

When I wake, the shadows dance with the light as the day turns to dusk and I feel the cool leather against my cheek. For a moment I think I'm back at home in the mansion with Tobias—my brother. A sudden dart of worry pierces my heart and I sit up quickly, only to find a gentle hand reaching out and a gruff voice say, "Relax, darlin', you're safe."

Turning, I see Maverick sitting beside me looking like hell and I stare at him in concern as he rakes his fingers through his hair and stares at me with pain-filled eyes. To my surprise, my first thought is of him and reaching out, I do something I've never had the bravery to do before and lightly stroke his cheek, saying with concern, "Tell me what's wrong."

He almost flinches under my touch and it makes me draw my hand back quickly as if it burns and I feel like a fool. He doesn't want me to touch him, it's obvious, he is just doing his job, after all.

As I look down, he reaches across and lifts my face to his and the fierce fire that blazes back at me makes me catch my breath as he growls, "What's wrong, darlin', is that everything's changed."

I feel the panic setting in as I sense change and wonder if he's having second thoughts about helping me. It must show in my expression because he groans and pulls me close once again and whispers against my hair, "I'm not sure you're safe with me. This was a bad idea."

My first thought is to run because the fear of rejection is too much to bear because he is the first man I have ever opened up to and it's obviously sickened him, so I make to pull away and he holds on tight, growling, "You're going nowhere."

"But..."

"You think I'm done with you, you're wrong. You think your sorry tale has put me off, you're wrong. You think you're on your own, you're so wrong. The reason everything's changed is because *we've* changed. How can I walk away now? How can I turn my back on something that stirred feelings inside me I never knew were possible for me? When you opened up to me, Sophia, it triggered a reaction that I never saw coming. Watching you sleep, cemented a feeling I knew as soon as I saw you in the forest. Your problem is *my* problem and that is why everything's changed. I don't want this, hell, I've been running from it for as many painful years as I can remember. I let no one in and that's just the way I like it. But you—you're different and that is what I'm finding so hard to reason with. You see, Sophia Moretti, you are trouble for me and I don't like trouble. My first instinct is to run. Take off and never look back."

"Then why don't you?"

My heart beats so fast it's like a pressure cooker building steam and once again I feel an incredible urge to do something I've never done before. So, with a bravery that comes from nowhere, I stare at those malevolent eyes and whisper, "Will you help me, Maverick?"

I can see he's conflicted and fighting an inner battle that I can only watch from afar, praying the right emotion will win in the end because I want something from him, I never thought I'd ask for.

His breathing is erratic and any control he once had is hanging by a thread as he says gruffly, "What do you want from me, Sophia?"

Closing my eyes tightly shut, I press my lips to his before I can change my mind and for a moment, I think he's going to pull away. There's a slight hesitation and yet I keep my mouth pressed to his until he groans and grabs the back of my head and grinds his lips to mine in an act of pure desperation. My lips part as he forces them open and as his tongue enters my mouth and claims its territory, I feel a shiver pass through me that ignites a fire inside that has been waiting its whole life for a spark. His scent fills my senses and his rough stubble grazes my skin, reminding me this man is no gentleman, he's rough, dirty and feral and it feels amazing.

Then he pulls back and it's like a bucket of icy water dousing the flames as he tears away and groans, "This isn't right."

Once again, I feel the rejection and the tears burn as I say in a small voice, "Then I'll go."

I make to stand and a hand shoots out and grasps my wrist so hard I wince with the pain and he says roughly, "I said you're going nowhere. What I mean is, this isn't right because you have just told me something that changes things. I don't want to be another monster taking advantage of a young innocent girl. That's not what happens here. You trusted me and I'll not take advantage of that. The thing is, you have asked for something I am only too eager to follow through for my own selfish reasons. But not now, not under these circumstances and not until you are sure."

"But…" His hand silences my mouth and his eyes soften into two liquid pools of desire mixed with yearning. "I want you Sophia, so badly I don't know what to do about it. My greatest fear is that you won't want me when you know the truth and so I'm shutting this down now, before either of us gets hurt. I'll not be the man who takes advantage of a young girl who doesn't know what dancing with the devil involves, so settle back and I'll give you that food I promised and you can tell me why the fuck you think you killed your parents."

His words bring me back to reality and I slump back against the seat and feel the pain twist inside me like an angry knife that just won't go away. He reaches across and grabs a plate filled with a sandwich and some potato chips and says huskily, "Eat, there's some water here to keep a clear head. You're to eat and tell me the rest, so we can work out what we're gonna do about it."

I nod with an acceptance that surprises me. He wants me to open up to him and I thought I already had. But he wants it all. The whole sorry tale and the bare bones of my soul. He will not rest until I have shared something with him of which I'm not sure I can form the words, let alone say out loud, so while I eat, I try to work out how on earth I'm going to get through the night ahead.

CHAPTER 9

MAVERICK

Watching Sophia eat is torture of the worst kind. Every mouthful she takes reminds me of a very different thing we could be doing right now, but I'm not ready for that. The fact she's even here is going against every instinct I have because Sophia Moretti is my ruin. She just doesn't know that yet and I'm the fucking idiot for letting her bring me down.

She finishes up and hands me the plate gratefully. "Thank you, I didn't realize how hungry I was."

Our fingers brush as I take the plate and that one simple act causes every nerve in me to stand to attention.

Setting it down on the side table, I say gruffly, "So, what happened next?"

She looks down and my first instinct is to grab her hand and hold it in mine, squeezing it with a reassurance she badly needs.

Sighing, she says in a sad voice, "I waited for Carlos for the whole day and night. I thought he'd gone for food, but it soon became obvious he wasn't coming back. His bag was gone and I felt like such a fool it took me so long to register that simple fact. I was destroyed, Maverick. I felt used, dirty and like a cheap whore who surrendered something so valuable to a monster. I hated myself more than him and that feeling has never left me. After a while, I faced the facts and called a cab to take me home. The trouble was, as soon as I got there, I knew something bad had happened."

She breaks off and puts her head in her hands and the grief visits her for a second wave. I rub her back and say nothing because she needs to deal with this in her own way.

"There were so many guards, I knew immediately something bad had happened. They were running around with an urgency that was different. Once the cab stopped, I was told to go inside and not look back. As soon as I stepped foot inside the door, my brother Tobias was there looking so angry I feared for my life. I thought he'd found out what happened and was disgusted with me. He was - just not for the reason I thought. He grabbed my hand and dragged me upstairs to our parent's room. I was so scared, but he said nothing until he opened the door and ushered me inside."

She looks up and the terror in her eyes shows me she's back in that room as she breaks. "There was so much blood. It was everywhere. It looked as if something had been butchered in my parent's room. Blood on the walls, the carpet and on the silken sheets. I remember retching as I struggled to breathe and Tobias gripped my face and made me look, telling me I had done this."

She starts to sob and my murderous rage transfers to her brother this time. Fucking bastard. But I know him. I know the man he is and that's what hurts the most. I understand him.

Then she raises her eyes to mine and says in a whisper, "Then he dragged me downstairs to my father's den where it was a similar scene. Blood absolutely everywhere, even more than upstairs it seemed. Then he yelled at me that Carlos had used the information I fed him against us. While Tobias and Thomas our other brother were out, he had stormed the mansion with his men and killed everyone in their path. There was no warning and no time to defend themselves. When Tobias and Thomas returned home, they found a bloodbath. Thomas was out seeking revenge and as it happens, returned to us in the worst way possible."

Now she's shivering as the ghosts of her past hold her captive and she says in a painful voice, "He arrived in pieces inside a plastic bag. Dumped at the gates like a pile of trash as a stark reminder of everything that is bad with our world."

She looks at me with a haunted expression and says with a quiver to her voice, "Maverick. The pain was too much to deal with. I thought my heart was going to give out on me because it tore me apart. However, it was nothing like the pain Tobias felt because I saw him break before my eyes. You see, Thomas was his twin, they were part of each other and a part of Tobias died along with him that day and it was all my fault. I had given the monster the keys to our door and let him blow it apart with the worst kind of explosion."

For some reason, as the last word leaves her lips, she changes before my eyes. The mask slips back in place and any emotion is shut tightly behind it. In a hard voice, she says bitterly. "We all changed that day. There was no light in our life, just the darkness. Tobias went on a killing spree and slaughtered every member of the Toledo family - personally. He bathed in their blood and had no mercy. He was a beast whose hunger never left him. Revenge became the air that he breathed and I thought I had lost him too.

Then it turned out that the only man left standing was the one responsible. Carlos Toledo was the man who escaped time and time again, and when he returned, it was to finish what he started."

Sophia looks at me with the blank expression of a woman

who has lost it all. I can tell she is broken all the way to her core and she shakes her head and says with a voice devoid of emotion. "I'm sorry, Maverick, but I can't deal with what happened next. I'm not ready for that. Maybe I never will be, but thank you for hearing me out. Now you know what a monster I am. I live in a world where life has no meaning. I'm a pampered princess who was never given the option to live a normal life. I deserve everything that I have to live with because of my own stupidity. If Carlos is dead, which I'm pretty sure he must be right now, I'm only sorry it wasn't by my hand. You see, I'm a monster of the worst kind and should be left to rot with my own tainted memories because I don't deserve to live, when I have ruined the lives of so many."

She nods and stands and says in a hollow voice. "Thanks for your help but I'll be going now. I need to be on my own."

As she makes for the door, I spring into action. God only knows what possesses me to do what I do next but I can't let her leave like this—like she's the one responsible and so, I reach out and spin her against my body and lock her against me tightly. With a growl, I fist her hair and grind my lips to hers and devour those lips that spilled such devastation and claim them for my own. I press her against me and hold her there until the thin fabric of our clothes becomes an irritation and I growl, "You're going nowhere, darlin'. You see, you and I are two of a kind. You think I'm some kind of knight in shining armor. You think my hands are clean, well, newsflash, baby, I'm a fucking killer. I have killed more men than your brothers combined and I would do it all over again if it meant cleaning the streets of trash like Carlos Toledo. You think I judge you because of your story—wrong. I live with my own nightmares and you will learn to do the same. People like us are survivors, darlin' and you will find a strength inside you that helps you deal with what happened.

Just for the record though, you killed no one. Your family knew the risks involved in living the life they did. If Carlos was allowed inside your mansion, it was because your parents failed to protect themselves, not because of any information you gave out. You think I don't know the life you lead? I know it more than most."

"How?"

She pulls back and looks at me with many questions burning in her eyes and I shake my head. "I don't do mafia, honey. I don't want anything to do with them and I have my own reasons for that. This isn't about me though; it's about you and you are not leaving until I say so."

"You can't keep me here."

My heart lifts as I see the woman she was trained to be resurface and push the frightened girl away. Those green eyes flash with a superiority that reminds me of the mafia princess she is. The anger clouds her expression and makes me laugh inside. Sophia Moretti is a warrior, she has just lost sight of that for a while, so I growl, "You asked me to help you and I will. Now, what do you want me to do first?"

I already know her answer by the way she lifts her head defiantly and looks me straight in the eye and says firmly, "Show me how it was supposed to be."

I feel the beast inside me roar as she stares at me with a challenge in those beautiful green eyes. I know that if I reject her now, she would suffer more in the long term, so I need to be careful with what I do next.

Lifting my hand to her face, I gently stroke the contours of her beautiful face and whisper softly, "You don't want that, beautiful. You want the fairy tale. I'm not the prince in that, I'm the beast you should avoid at all costs."

"I don't want a prince; I've been a princess all my life and I'm tired of her. I want no strings, no emotion, just sex. I want someone to show me how amazing it can be and make me a woman to drive away the frightened girl inside. I want you to be that man because you are the only man I have ever trusted outside my own family. If you don't want to, I'll understand but I need to ask, will you fuck me, Maverick and give me my life back?"

CHAPTER 10

SOPHIA

As soon as the words left my lips, I think I held my breath. Who is this woman inside me? I have never asked a man to fuck me - ever, but I want this man to, more than I want to breathe and if he rejects me, then I'll be crushed.

He looks at me and a thousand reasons why he should send me packing pass through his eyes and I stand facing him, willing him to put me out of my misery. From the moment I met him, I felt a sexual attraction to him I've never felt with anyone before. Unlike my brother, I have shied away from physical contact with the opposite sex. Tobias became a sex addict and craved the contact with a willing female, that is until he met Anastasia and discovered he wanted a different kind of relationship. I don't. I want the sex. The physical contact and the release that will give me. I want to channel my feelings into passion and drive the demons away. I want it to be the warrior who stands like a beast before me with his rough, crude tongue and wild manner. I need a strong man, nothing like the men I live among. I need someone so far removed from all that to set me on the right path and so I wait nervously for his decision as he battles with his own reasons why he should turn me away.

Then he speaks. "I'll help you, Sophia, but not like this."

I blink in shock and he cups my face in both his hands and stares deeply into my soul. "I will not fuck you; you deserve better than that. I will show you what it's like to be loved by a man and then I will walk away. No strings attached and no emotions involved. Just pleasure. Those are my terms and are non-negotiable. Think on it and let me know your decision."

"I accept."

He laughs softly, "Don't you want some time to think about it?"

I lick my lips nervously and his eyes darken. "No, I need it to be now because we have come too far to turn back."

He nods and leans down and touches my lips with his with a feather light touch. This time it's different. It's soft and sexy and sends a tingle through me that builds the anticipation.

For a while, we just stand and kiss, slowly, seductively and with the promise of what's coming.

Then he pulls away and I am shocked by the softness in his eyes as he whispers huskily, "Come with me."

I take his hand and let him lead me to a door set in the corner of the room. My heart hammers inside as I prepare myself for something I'm not sure I want a repeat performance of.

As we walk into Maverick's bedroom, I swallow hard as I look at the huge bed dominating the center of the room dressed in silken simplicity.

He turns to me and says gently, "Do you want to shower and check this is still what you want?"

"I know it's what I want."

He nods. "Then we will do this together, on your terms. Anytime you want me to stop, you say the word and I need you to know I will. Don't be afraid of that because I'm not gonna hurt you, understand?"

I nod and shiver with anticipation. I can't believe this is happening. Finally, and with a man like him.

I watch as Maverick steps back and reaching for his top lifts it cleanly off, standing before me bare chested and I can do nothing but stare. His muscles ripple against the tattoos that cover them, reminding me just who he is. The Grim Reaper mocks me as it stares back at me, reminding me of the killer he is and the killer I am in a roundabout way. Two people who know the bitterness of death suffered in the most horrific of ways.

Reaching out, I touch the face of the instrument of darkness and draw a deep breath as I press my lips to it; embracing it and making it my own. I will not fear death anymore. It's an inevitable part of life and we owe it to ourselves to avoid it for as long as possible, but it's always there - waiting. Maverick tenses under my lips and I feel him shudder against me. Raising my eyes to his, I am shocked at the power in those eyes looking down at me containing the blackest storm. He steps back and I watch as he removes his belt and lowers his jeans to the floor, standing before me naked and unashamed.

"What no pants?"

I make a joke because seeing Maverick hard and ready for battle makes me tremble with need. I feel a slick feeling between my legs and my pussy throbs with an urgent need. It's calling to him and I marvel at how natural this is.

Without saying another word, I lift my own shirt above my head and toss it to the ground, before shrugging out of my skirt. I stand before him in just my underwear and a wish for him to make this count.

He does nothing and yet the look on his face is one of hunger. He wants to eat me alive, it's there in his expression and gives me a bravery I need right now to finish the job. I unclasp my bra and shimmy out of my panties and stand before him as nature intended. Still no words are spoken, just loaded promises that hang in the air between us as I wait for him to show me what I've been missing out on. Then he takes my hand and leads me to the bed and grabbing my shoulders, sits me on the edge before kneeling at my feet. Then he growls, "I want to worship at your feet like the servant I am."

His hands spread my knees apart and inches me slightly forward until I am open before him. I should feel embarrassed but I don't, just curious. His face turns against my most private part and I feel his tongue flick against my clit which should disgust me but it doesn't. His thumbs part the folds that guard it so well and he takes it into his mouth and sucks gently, causing me to wriggle as the most delicious feeling spreads through my body. His tongue licks and teases as I grind against his face unashamedly and without care. It feels so good and I moan as the pressure builds. It feels so wrong and yet so intoxicating I almost can't breathe, and then he pushes me back against the bed and positions himself above me. Then he leans down and kisses me and I taste my desire on his tongue. It feels hot and dirty and I can't get enough of it.

Then he kisses a trail down my face and sucks at my neck, biting and scraping the delicate flesh with his teeth.

I groan some more and feel his fingers edge lower and flick my clit with a sharpness that causes me to gasp and the wetness between my legs leaves a slippery trail that will help him inside. He rubs his cock against my opening and I wrap my legs around his waist and he whispers, "Are you sure you want this, honey?"

"Oh god, yes."

He laughs against my chest as he sucks a nipple between his teeth and bites gently, causing me to moan a little louder. He growls, "Moan for me baby, moan my name and beg for it."

It should feel wrong but it doesn't as I groan loudly, "Fuck me, Maverick, please, I want you so badly."

His fingers trace a path between my legs and he pushes them wider and laughs as I move up to meet him. I grind my pussy on his hand and feel so much heat tearing me apart. His fingers find their way inside and the hard friction causes me to pant with a desperation I have never felt before. "Please, I want more."

I don't care that I'm begging him, that doesn't matter right now; what does is finishing what we've started because I'm like a greedy whore who can't get enough. His fingers curl inside me and stroke me gently at first, then with an increased rhythm and I feel the pressure building as I buck against his hand, but it's not enough. I want all of him, so I plead, "I want to feel you inside me, please."

I'm only half aware that he reaches across and opens the drawer beside his bed and grabs a condom, tearing it from the packet with his teeth. I don't even register the time he takes to protect us both while I lie waiting, a quivering mess of desire and excitement, craving what comes next more than life itself.

Then he leans down and kisses me hard and deep and with a passion that brings out the wild animal inside me, as he turns into a raging beast igniting a passion in me I never thought I had. Fisting his hair in my hands, I cry out, "Now, please, do it now."

He needs no further invitation and thrusts in hard causing my pussy to clench and I cry out. Suddenly, he stops and whispers, "You ok, darlin'?"

"Yes." I gasp as I realize I am. It doesn't hurt, just a feeling of being so full I can't move. Maverick is inside my mind, body and soul and I never want him to leave. It's like a drug I need to survive and as he starts to move gently inside me, I feel him claim every part of me as he moves a little faster and then with an urgency that sends me over the edge. I dig my nails into his back as I scream his name, over and over again as he claims me as his. It's rough, dirty and frantic and my sweat runs like a river that's burst its banks as his balls slap against my ass and my legs wrap around his waist, bringing him deeper inside. He groans and says roughly, "Fuck, baby, that feels so good. Dig harder."

I scrape my nails deeper and relish the gasp of pleasure that springs from his lips and reaching down cup his balls and hang on for grim death. I want all of him. I want to make this count. I want him so deep rooted inside me I swallow him whole. I need him to fuck me completely and fuck the images from my mind of the one who went before him. I only want to see him when I close my eyes at night and I need him to be brutal and claim my black soul.

We go on the ride of our life and I don't know where this woman came from. I'm like a wild animal, an insatiable being that can't get enough. He rolls to his back and pulls me up until I sit impaled on him and holding my hips gently rocks me against him so he fills every part of me. He grabs my breast like a hungry animal and sucks it till it hurts. I groan like a woman possessed and I am. By him. My clit drags against his shaft as I take him in deeper and won't allow him out. I need him so badly and never want this to end. If this is my one chance at feeling, then I am making it count.

But my body has other ideas and suddenly it explodes with a feeling so intoxicating, I want it to last for ever. As Maverick roars, I scream so hard they must hear us in space as I clench his cock between my thighs and ride a wave like an accomplished surfer right to the end.

His arm reaches out and pulls me down hard against his chest and he kisses my hair and whispers, "You ok, baby?"

I'm shocked to feel the hot, wet tears leak to his cheeks as I come apart against him. He rubs my back and holds me tenderly and yet in the tightest embrace, as I lose total control and break down in his arms.

After a while, he whispers, "I hope those are happy tears, darlin'."

I laugh against his chest with him still inside me and whisper, "Thank you. Thank you for showing me how amazing it can be. I will never be able to thank you enough."

He continues to stroke my hair and says gruffly, "It's only amazing because of you. That was special; you need to know that."

I pull back and look at him in surprise and he strokes my cheeks and says gruffly. "Listen, baby, I've had sex more than hot dinners and it has *never* been like that. That was the best, *you* are the best and I want you to know that. It counted and now the only thing we have to worry about is that now I've found you, I doubt I'll let you leave my side."

He pulls my lips to his and kisses me so sweetly it blows my mind. Then as I lay my head on his chest and his arms wrap around me, I know just what he means. Nothing can ever be better than this, I'm finally here, I belong.

CHAPTER 11

MAVERICK

Now I'm screwed in every way possible. I wasn't kidding when I told her I wasn't letting her leave. How the fuck did this happen? That was the best sex of my entire life and it was because it was with her. Sophia Moretti. The woman I was always meant to find. As I cradle her in my arms, the situation hits home. I never wanted this—a woman. I'm a loner, best on my own, but now I couldn't let her go if I tried. Will she look at me differently when she finds out my dirty little secret? Will she regret letting me in because she has every right to be pissed? She's not the only one with secrets and mine threatens to blow her world apart.

As usual, I push the problem away to deal with another day. This is our day, mine and Sophia's and now I need to show her how good it can be.

Sophia sighs and rolls to her side and says sadly, "Thanks, Maverick."

Turning to face her, I lean on one elbow and play with her hair. "No thanks needed; I should be the one thanking you."

Her lip trembles and once again the fear enters her eyes as she whispers, "I should go."

"Where?"

She laughs a little self-consciously. "Maybe have a shower, grab some sleep, you know, the usual."

"What's wrong with doing that here?"

She looks surprised and I see a little of the fear lift from her eyes. "But I thought…"

"That it was a once in a lifetime opportunity, just business? Think again, darlin' because I meant what I said back there. Things have changed and I want more."

She smiles shyly and I watch in fascination as her whole face lights up. "Really?"

Leaning in, I kiss that heavenly mouth and whisper, "Forget what I said before, get your stuff, you're moving in."

"And if I say no?"

"Then I'll do it for you. You see, when you make a deal with the devil, he kind of changes the rules as he goes along and you're never free. Time to honor your agreement because I meant every word I said back there, you're staying - end of conversation."

Her eyes fill with tears and she smiles softly, "Thank you."

"For what?"

"For caring enough to try. Nobody ever has and it means so much."

She sits up and pulls the sheet to cover her breasts and says sadly, "I've always been alone. I was the pampered daughter of a Mafia Don. My two brothers made it impossible for me to mix with outsiders and I was guarded wherever I went. I met Carlos through school and we managed to keep it to ourselves for quite some time. Nobody else even tried to get close to me because it wasn't worth the physical injury involved. When we lost our parents, Tobias became worse. I was by his side through the day and retreated to my room at night. If I went out, it was with the guards and none of them so much as looked at me in a different way because they knew the consequences if they did. So, you see, Maverick, nobody ever thought I was worth fighting for. I suppose when you grow up in those circumstances you start to believe it yourself. But you, you tried. You didn't take no for an answer and the saddest thing of all, is that I've spoken more to you than anyone in the last five years. My brother wasn't interested in what I did when I wasn't with him. He was too busy getting screwed by his whores, or beating his enemies to a pulp. My only friend was our housekeeper, Mrs. Billings, and I don't even call her by her first name. So, I'm sorry I was an easy lay and didn't play hard to get like the women most men prefer. I'm sorry I gave it up like the many whores you're used to, but you see, I never got many opportunities to play those games myself. If you think badly of me, then I'm sorry for that too, but I'm not sorry for what we just did. If it was the one and only time, I will not feel bad about that because finally I have seen first-hand what the fuss is all about."

Sitting up to face her, I draw her lips to mine and taste the sweet lips of a woman I never thought I'd find. Yes, I've had many others before her, but none came close to stirring actual feelings inside me. That's what makes her special and what makes her mine.

As I lower her down on the bed, once again I show her what that means to me, and by the time the night is over, I will have shown her over and over again.

∼

5.30 AM and I'm wide awake. Sophia is sleeping peacefully beside me and it seems a shame to wake her. She must be exhausted because I was intent on proving how much she meant to me all fucking night long. It was as if I couldn't get enough. Any moment when part of me wasn't in contact with her was immediately rectified and if anyone deserves to rest, it's her. But I have other plans and gently shake her awake, "Come on, darlin', no slacking."

"What time is it?" She rubs her eyes and I'm in two minds whether to break with my routine and indulge in a different form of exercise but figure she needs the rest, so say firmly, "It's time to take that morning run."

"Really?"

Her eyes snap open wide in disbelief and I laugh softly. "I need you in top condition to keep up with me and it starts today. Now, unless you want to join me and run naked, save for a pair of shorts, I suggest you head back to your room and meet me in ten outside."

Groaning, she pulls herself up and shakes her head. "Fine, have it your way."

"Oh, I will, darlin' and I'll have it again and again and again."

I wink and she rolls her eyes, laughing softly. How I love the sound of it and love the fact her eyes are filled with a sparkle that wasn't there before. Sophia is starting to come to life before my eyes and it's an incredible sight.

She leaves and I jump in the shower to wash away a night of passion that equaled no other. It felt good and nothing like I thought it would. Normally as soon as I fuck a woman, I'm keen for her to leave. Hardly chivalrous I know, but I'm not interested in them past the obvious. Millie was always accommodating but started to make demands that were never on offer. She'll be pissed when she sees me with Sophia, but I can't help that. I never pretended we were anything but what normally happens between a biker and whore.

Most of the girls here love the freedom that gives them.

They are all here for their own reasons and nobody expects anything from them they aren't prepared to give. We treat them well and they want for nothing. Those who do make it to an old lady, live like a queen. Some of the whores move on, but only when they're ready. If Millie had designs on being my old lady, it was never gonna happen. I made that crystal clear over the time I've been here and made sure to choose different girls to drive the message home. But now, if so much as one of the other bikers looks at Sophia, they will find out what lengths I go to protect my property and the sooner they know that she is—my property, the better because the minute she starts mixing in, then she will be fair game for the whole fucking lot of them.

CHAPTER 12

SOPHIA

So, this is considered the walk of shame. I giggle to myself as I steal through the night as carefully as possible, so as not to disturb the other bikers sleeping nearby. Quietly, I creep through the yard toward the building where the women live and can't quite believe I'm the same woman who went jogging just yesterday. So much has happened and all of it good because of one man.

First the jog, then the ice-cream, ending up with one emotion filled night, followed by the best sex I could ever have dreamed of having. I cannot wait to repeat the performance and marvel at how quickly my life has changed in the space of just a few hours.

By the time I reach my room, I am wide awake and eager to start my day. What will this one bring? More of the same I hope and I wonder if Maverick was joking when he asked me to move in with him. Live with a man, that's serious stuff and so, as I shower and change, I can't get back there quickly enough.

He's already waiting as I make my way outside and I roll

my eyes as I see his bare chest calling to me. "What, no top —again?"

"Told you, honey, that's just unnecessary laundry."

As I reach his side, he pulls me in fast and hard against him and kisses me deeply. My arms reach for him and I kiss him back with a hunger I never had before and as my body inches closer, I feel my nipples straining against the thin lycra top. Reaching under it, Maverick rolls my nipple in his finger and bites my bottom lip before squeezing my ass hard and growls, "I want you to work up a sweat a different way before I tie you to my bed and fuck you deeply for the rest of the day."

His wicked mouth excites me way too much and as I break away and start running, I shout over my shoulder, "You'll have to catch me first."

I start to run in the direction of the trees and laugh as I hear him gaining on me behind. I know I'll never out run him, but it's a game I'm keen to play. Maybe I push myself a little too hard because the sweat drenches my vest and my breathing is hard as I gasp for oxygen. Then the air is knocked out of my lungs as he scoops me back and pushes me to the forest floor. A bed of leaves provide the only comfort as he pushes my vest over my breasts and leans down and sucks each one roughly and without care. I arch into him and run my hands over his dripping body and groan as he rips my shorts down in one swift move. His soon follow and as my legs wrap around his waist, he thrusts inside and I gasp as I feel the full force of the man himself with no barrier between us.

"But…"

"Don't worry, baby, I'll pull out. I just want to feel you with nothing between us."

Feeling Maverick's cock inside me, excites me way too much and I moan his name as he rocks inside me, thrusting so hard the leaves and twigs tear at my skin. I start panting as we mate like wild animals, not caring who else is around and, as he holds my arms above my head, I love the whole primal sexiness of this dirty encounter. He growls in my ear, "Come for me, baby, show me you're mine."

I need no further invitation because I scream his name as I clench his cock and squeeze it hard and as he pulls out just in time, I love feeling the hot, sweet sticky jets of his own orgasm shoot all over my breasts and chest.

The fact it's still half dark makes it even more dangerous and as the sweat coats our bodies, I pant and gasp for air. Grabbing a handful of leaves, Maverick wipes the sticky mess from my chest and pulls my top down over my engorged breasts. Then he pulls up my shorts and kisses me lightly on the lips, saying huskily, "Now you'd better run faster than that if you don't want to see what happens next."

He stands up and pulls me with him and then smacks me hard on my ass and says roughly, "I'll give you a head start."

Giggling, I head off at a pace and don't even care this is against every single one of my feminist principles. He could tie me to a tree and whip me with a branch and I couldn't be happier to let him. You see, Maverick can do no wrong in my eyes because he has made me the center of his world right now and for someone who has never had that, it's a powerful force.

An hour later and I am bruised, sore and swollen and all of its good. Despite the extreme sex run, I wouldn't have wanted it any other way. Maverick used the time to help me with some other kind of moves and for a while there, we were playing the game of assailant and victim. He showed me ways to defend myself should anyone try to take me again and as I learned a few tricks; I began to feel a little braver.

As I head inside to shower and change before meeting

him back at his place for breakfast, I can't quite believe my luck that he has come into my life.

On my way out to meet him, I bump into the girl who greeted him so warmly yesterday morning and she smiles sweetly as I pass, before saying, "How are things, honey?"

I return the smile and nod. "Things are good thanks."

"You seem a little brighter, are things calming down a little?"

"Yes, thank you. I feel a little happier because yesterday I went into town for the first time and learned a few self defense moves."

She looks interested. "That sounds good, who helped you?"

I feel a little anxious and just say shyly, "Maverick."

"Oh."

Immediately her face falls and I wonder if I've missed something here. Remembering the way she flew into his arms, tells me there's something more going on and I feel bad.

She smiles but I can tell her mind is elsewhere and I say softly, "I'm sorry, is Maverick your guy?"

Her eyes widen and she shakes her head vigorously. "God, no. I mean, I wouldn't say no if he asked, but they never do. Ask, that is."

I feel bad for her and she laughs self-consciously. "It's fine, I know the score. The guys I mix with are just looking for a distraction most of the time. Me too if I'm honest but sometimes it's hard not to feel more, do you get what I'm saying?"

Now I feel bad and nod. "It must be hard."

"Don't get me wrong, Sophia, I love my life here. The guys are great and it's not a chore going with them. I don't know why I want Maverick as much as I do. He has never promised me anything but a good time and yet he's something else entirely. There's something edgy about him that's mixed with a lost feeling that makes me wonder what happened in his life before he came here."

Now I'm interested and whisper, "How did he get to come here?"

"Not sure really." She shrugs. "Most of them are ex-military or along those lines. Maverick isn't, that much I do know. The thing is, he keeps his cards close guarded and isn't one for answering questions."

She looks at me and half smiles. "Anyway, I should be heading in, it's been one of those nights."

It strikes me that she's not dressed for breakfast and appears to be wearing last night's clothes, judging by the look of her smudged eyes, and she grins as she sees me looking. "Don't you worry about me, honey, I had the best night. Razor's back and starved of female company. He was out of control, which is just how I like them."

She winks and heads off and I feel a surge of pity for the attractive girl. She deserves someone who makes her feel like a queen, not used by the men here because even though she pretends it's what she wants, I can see the yearning for more behind those pretty eyes.

However, her mentioning Maverick sets me on edge. What's he hiding behind and why is he here? She's right, he keeps things close, hell, so do I but if I'm going to trust him with my darkest secrets, then he should trust me, surely that's how it works.

CHAPTER 13

MAVERICK

As runs go, that was the best of my life and I have the pretty lady to thank for that. She was a willing student in every way and against my better judgment, I am enjoying every second I spend with the delectable Miss Moretti. That alone has surprised me because she is so different to how I imagined. There's a hard edge that shows itself once in a while but behind it, she's soft, feminine and has a quick wit that I want to help her sharpen. She has the makings of a great woman and I want to be the man on the receiving end of that. Two days ago, I wanted nothing to do with her. Now I'm thinking up ways to keep her.

I can tell something's up the minute she walks into my apartment and I say roughly, "What happened?"

She looks up in surprise and tries to wave it off. "Oh, nothing, it's silly really."

"I'll be the judge of that."

I walk toward her and she looks down, which rings the alarm bells. Reaching her, I lift her face to mine and say firmly, "Tell me."

"It's nothing. I met up with one of the um... ladies and she made me think on a few things I shouldn't."

"What did she say?"

I'm curious because I'm not sure what anyone could say that would worry Sophia so much and she shakes herself and laughs self-consciously. "She told me you were hiding behind something and it got me thinking."

I can't speak because she is so close to the truth, I can't let my guard slip for an instant.

"What about?"

"Me, I suppose. Ever since I came here, I've been hiding behind a secret. I haven't told anyone because quite honestly, that secret will be my downfall. But you, it hurts me so much to think you have to live with something you can't explain. I want to help you the same as you helped me, but I don't know how. I'm not one to give advice, but I want a shot at least."

"There's nothing to tell." I sigh with exasperation and say bluntly, "Whoever told you that is stirring the pot unnecessarily. You've got to know that some of these whores would give anything to be in your shoes. They will say and do anything to cause trouble because it makes their lives seem less meaningless."

She stares at me in shock. "Meaningless; you hypocrite."

"Maybe I am but I speak the truth."

She looks to be thinking on what I say and then snaps. "You can hold the breakfast because I've lost my appetite. I should get to work."

She turns away and I reach out and pull her back, saying with frustration, "Don't walk away from me in anger—ever. If you have a problem with me, we talk it out. You may not like what goes on here, darlin' but it works. If a whore is filling your head with shit, then it's up to you to process the information and make your own decisions. What should matter is how I treat you and I'm telling you; I have never spent the night with a woman and certainly not in my bed. I do not make food for them and I do not spend time with them outside of when I'm inside them. So, if you don't like the way I put you higher than them, you've got a problem. As for me hiding, you're a fine one to talk. You still have some explaining to do and you know it's only a matter of time before you tell us the real reason you're hiding here. Until then, let me show you how to face your fears."

Sophia looks at me with so much disgust it makes me want to crawl into a pit and die. Her eyes narrow and she hisses. "Thanks for your help, but I'll be fine from now on. I'm not interested in spending time with a man who dismisses women so cruelly. For your information, that girl was sweet, honest and concerned. She wasn't stirring the pot as you say and seemed genuinely worried. Maybe it's best you go back to only enjoying women when you're inside them because quite honestly, your conversation sucks, anyway."

She spins on her heel and heads back the way she came and I make a fist. Fucking women, no wonder I keep away. I'll never understand what goes on inside their head—ever.

Like Sophia, I've lost my appetite and decide to punch it out on the bags in the gym.

She needs to cool down and realize that she's fighting over nothing.

～

As I punch the lights out of the bag, I hear someone laughing and look up to see Snake lifting some weights on the bench.

I glare at him and he grins. "Happens to us all bro."

"What?"

I'm cold and abrupt but I don't care and he shrugs.

"Women. They have a habit of getting under your skin and once they have, there's no shaking them. The ones with a brain are worse. They take no shit and make up their minds before knowing the facts. They're hot headed, full bodied and fiery as hell and you know what, they are the best kind."

I sigh with exasperation. "How did you know?"

"Been there, done that and ripped the t-shirt in half. You know my old lady, she ain't no pushover either and that little lady you're spending time with is a hard one to crack. From what I can see, you're doing a good job, so far, anyway, but you need to know when to back off."

"What are you an expert?"

"If I was, I'd charge you for my advice."

I roll my eyes as he grins. "Let her simmer down, she'll come back. You just need to learn that some battles are not worth fighting. For those that are, the victory is in the making up at the end. All that aside though, has she said anything about why she won't go home?"

Sinking down on the bench opposite, I shake my head wearily. "She's close but some stupid whore got in the way and filled her head with tales of me hiding something."

I can feel Snake's eyes penetrating deep inside me and then he shrugs. "You are."

"She doesn't need to know that, hell she'd better never find out."

"How's that gonna work? I mean, if she sticks around and you get close, it will come out one day and then you'll be deeper in shit than you would if you came clean now."

"NO!"

Snake shrugs. "It's your call to make. Anyway, my old lady is back today, so I'm off to make sure the house is tidy. Call me a pussy, but I kind of want to spend the night inside her, not cleaning my shit before she'll let me. You know, Maverick, it's the women that control the army, they are the generals and you are just there to obey their commands. We do so because the rewards are great and a happy old lady makes for an ecstatic old man. Whatever it is, it's not worth losing the honey for. Get what I'm saying."

He heads off and I punch the bench in despair. Fucking mafia, I knew I should have stayed away.

CHAPTER 14

SOPHIA

All morning I've been raging about Maverick and his crude way of talking. He was so dismissive of Millie and it showed a side to him that I didn't care for. Would he talk the same way about me when the shine wears off? Probably. However, there's a part of me that thinks I overreacted. I have no right to judge this life they lead. Just because it's different, it doesn't make it wrong. I've heard the girls swapping stories on the men they spend the night with. I hear them through the walls and through the crack in an open door. It intrigues and disgusts me in equal measures and I kind of want to find out for myself what goes on in that big barn they all head to every night without fail.

Thinking of Maverick working his way through them, doing things to them that he did to me, hurts like hell. Then the way he dismissed them as just a warm body to hide inside sickened me to my stomach. Is that what I am; am I a whore like the rest of them? I certainly acted like it but it was so good at the time. I don't even feel ashamed, just desperate for more. Is this what this place is, a den of iniquity that claims the morals and the souls of everyone inside?

"Penny for them, honey?"

I look up as Ashton watches me from the doorway, looking like an angel in a pale blue sundress.

She smiles as she heads toward me and sits beside me on the couch where I am holding Caspian as he sleeps. As I look down at his perfect face, my heart fills with love for him. So perfect and so innocent, how I wish he would stay this way.

As she sits beside me, I say sadly, "At what point in a man's life does he lose this pure innocence and become an…"

"Asshole?"

Ashton laughs and gazes fondly at her son. "I'm guessing they follow by example and honey, living here is a breeding ground for them."

I stare at her in surprise and she laughs. "These guys are a lot to deal with. They say and do things that no woman should hear because they forget there are boundaries. You know, when I first came here, I was scared out of my mind. Ryder took one look at me and made me marry him the same day. I didn't have a choice."

I stare at her in complete shock and she grins. "As it turns out, it was the best thing that ever happened to me. It took me a while to get accustomed to their ways and we had lots of disagreements along the way. But we got there and I wouldn't want to be anywhere else. You see, these men are hard, crude and rough but have all the ingredients to make a woman loyal, strong and happy. I'm guessing you've come across one of them yourself which is why you're struggling with your feelings."

"Is it that obvious?"

"Honey, we've all been where you are now. So, tell me, anyone I know?"

"Maverick."

Ashton looks interested and a slight smile ghosts her face before she nods. "I see your problem."

"He's like you said, an asshole."

"A hot asshole, mind."

Ashton grins and I can't help but laugh.

She strokes Caspian's gorgeous dark curls and says softly, "Maverick is, as his name suggests, a bit of a loner and a man who doesn't like to conform. He does what he wants, when he wants and I'm guessing if he has feelings for you, he is unaccustomed to them. Like most of the guys here, he's a rough diamond, breath-taking in its beauty and solid throughout but catch a sharp edge and you know about it. They lack the polish of most fine jewels but are more valuable in their rough glory. Maybe you should give each other time because if I know Maverick, he doesn't give much away and just the fact he's letting you in a little, tells me everything I want to know."

She reaches for her baby and as I watch him settle in her arms, I wonder how she got so wise. She's right of course, its early days for us and we have a lot to learn about each other. From the sounds of it, we're alike in many ways because like Maverick, I hold myself apart and let no one in.

Ashton brings me back to the conversation and says sweetly, "Why don't you come with me later to meet the rest of them?"

"The bar?"

I look at her in horror and she laughs. "It's not that bad, honey. A little daunting at first, but I'll be right beside you. Come and meet the other girls and they will tell you everything you want to know. Don't be put off by what you see because those girls are living the dream. When I first came here, the word 'whore' left a bad taste in my mouth. I felt it was so degrading and couldn't imagine why any girl would call herself one with the obvious pride these girls do. But you should know the guys are the biggest whores in this place because they need those women more than the girls need them. When they catch feelings, they stay true and loyal and that is the greatest prize there is."

I think about what she says and then remember Millie and ask Ashton about her. "One of the girls, Millie, told me she thinks Maverick is hiding something. It made me think and I asked him about it. He totally overreacted and we argued. He was so dismissive of her, but she was only being kind. I suppose it got my back up and made me wonder if he would be as dismissive of me in company."

Ashton looks concerned and sighs heavily. "Millie does have feelings for Maverick but they have never been reciprocated. I feel for her but it's her problem to deal with, not yours, or his. He has never given her the impression they could be anything more than the usual relationship they all share. She's a sweet girl, like you said, and will find her way. I'm guessing that Maverick isn't ready to talk about his past because I expect only Ryder and Snake possibly know what that is. I'm sure you understand that, honey, after all, you're hiding a few secrets of your own, aren't you?"

I look at her sharply and she smiles reassuringly. "It's fine, I don't mean you should tell anyone what they are until you're good and ready, but secrets have a habit of coming out when you least expect it. Maybe if you open up to Maverick, he will do the same. Who knows, it may bring you closer together?"

"Maybe, then again, I'm still angry with him. I don't think I'm ready for a heart to heart with him anytime soon."

"Then come with me tonight, show him you are a strong lady and don't need a man to hold your hand."

Against my better judgment, I nod slowly, "Ok, what time and where?"

"Come and call for me at 8. The kids will be in bed and Lou will watch them if I ask."

"Won't Ryder mind?"

I feel anxious because I'm guessing they like to spend their evenings together and Ashton smiles. "Oh, he'll be there, honey, he always is. He just doesn't have to be there with me. A little independence keeps these men on their toes and it will do him good to entertain himself for a while."

She winks and she rockets up in my estimation of her. Yes, Ryder King may be the hardest bastard that ever lived, but this woman has the measure of him. I'm guessing he would do anything she asks, which shows me where the real power lies in this place. Yes, the women rule this particular roost and that settles my mind. It's the opposite to where I come from, where the women do exactly what they're told at all times. This is so refreshing and gives me hope for a future I never thought was mine to enjoy.

CHAPTER 15

MAVERICK

My day goes from bad to worse because Ryder calls me in and sends me out with a few of the others to deal with another low life that's overstepped the mark. He was head of a trafficking ring that traded women for dollars. He got greedy though and was blackmailing some powerful suits who bought them, threatening to leak their involvement unless they paid him big time. The cops arrested him but he got off on a technicality and was just about to blow the cover of too many people in high office. We stormed his warehouse and destroyed all the evidence, finding underage girls locked like dogs in cages, drugged up to their eyeballs. Let's just say he suffered an unfortunate accident and by the time the authorities arrived, they found him hanging by his sorry neck in an apparent suicide. The sight of those women scared shitless caused the beast in me to roar and it doesn't get any better when I return to see Sophia dressed in a figure-hugging black dress, heading into the bar with Ashton.

Before I can even change, we need to debrief with Ryder

and Snake and it's hard to keep my head in business picturing Sophia loose in that fuckbarn.

"Good job men, I've tied up the red tape and the file is closed. Head off and grab a shower and a cool beer."

Snake jumps up quicker than most and Ryder rolls his eyes. "I'm guessing Bonnie's back."

"She sure is and she better be ready and waiting for me because you won't be seeing me for the next two days."

"More like two minutes." Brewer laughs causing the rest of us to jeer but Snake just winks. "Keep telling yourself that Brewer because it's what he tells his old lady on a daily basis. Two minutes my ass, you're a lightweight."

Brewer hold his hands up. "Do you honestly think my old lady would still be with me if it took two minutes? Watch and learn kids because there's a reason that woman puts up with me."

"I ain't watching shit, couldn't think of anything worse than watching you with your old lady. I need a willing professional, or two." Rebel winks and I roll my eyes as he says, "Coming, Mav, you've been avoiding that clubhouse since you got back and the girls are mighty pissed. Fancy joining me in a spot of…"

"Get the fuck out of here, the lot of you. and keep your depraved habits for the bedroom, I don't wanna hear it."

Ryder shakes his head as we head out and Rebel is right about one thing, I am going to the bar tonight but it's with only one woman in my sight and she had better not be in the same pissy mood she was in earlier because I have plans for the two of us that nobody else needs to know the details of.

∼

I THINK I break all records for showering and washing the blood from my hands. As soon as I head inside the door, I look for her and it takes me a while before I see her backed in a corner looking scared shitless. Ashton is beside her and two of the whores, Lauren and Josephine. Nice enough girls who couldn't scare a bug from their shoe, which makes me wonder why she's so afraid.

Our eyes connect across the space and even from here, I see the relief enter hers. She looks down and a flush creeps across her face which makes me start walking. I don't get far before Amy, one of the whores grabs a hold and purrs, "Maverick, honey, I heard you were back, fancy hooking up with me tonight?"

"Not tonight, darlin'."

She shrugs and then turns her attention to another guy like an off/on switch and I carry on walking. I see Millie looking miserable behind the bar and feel a little bad for her. It's obvious she's upset, but if I go there, it's admitting I've done something wrong and I haven't. I've fucked Millie just as many times as any other girl here. There was no understanding between us and if she thought otherwise, it's in her head.

Ashton looks up and smiles when we approach and says in her soft, sweet voice, "Maverick, you're back. Did it go well?"

I nod respectfully. "Yes, Ryder's on his way, just finishing up."

She smiles and as her eyes move past me, I watch in awe as her pretty face softens and her expression changes to one of total devotion. We all know that look and crave it more than the air we breathe to see such a look directed at us. Ryder and Ashton have a love that is so pure it gives hope to the rest of us. If I was hoping for that same look from Sophia, I am mightily disappointed because as I look, her eyes narrow and she turns away, staring at her drink as if she can't stand the sight of me.

Lauren and Josephine watch with interest and one look from me has them scooting back down the bar. Ashton stands and says pleasantly, "Sorry guys, I'll just grab a minute with Ryder, will you be ok, Sophia?"

"I'll be fine, thanks, Ashton."

Her voice is soft with a hint of steel lacing it and Ashton catches my eye and looks almost apologetic. "Keep my seat warm, Maverick, I won't be long."

As she heads off, I take her seat and feel like a high school kid asking a girl to prom. It feels awkward as fuck and I'm in unknown territory. I'm not sure how to play this, so just say softly, "We need to talk."

She looks up and the sight of the pain in her eyes makes me want to smash something. Did I put that pain there, I sure as hell hope not?

She nods and then she looks around nervously and I see the sweat building on her upper lip as she appears to be having a panic attack before my eyes. Looking around, I finally understand.

This place is heaving and a lot to process when you see it for the first time. The guys are loud and fill the space with a dominant edge. The girls are at their worst when they are in this mood and openly make out on couches and against the walls. It's noisy, rough and the loud rock music does little to help the situation. There is cheering, jeering and loud laughter. Groaning, moaning and the sound of breaking glass. Some of the guys are openly staring at Sophia because she is fresh meat they are hungry for and instinctively I shield her a little from their view and throw a warning look to anyone who dares look in her direction.

Taking her hand, I'm happy to see she grips it hard and I feel her shake a little, so I lean in and whisper, "We should leave."

She just nods and so I pull her after me and head for the

door, stopping only to tell Ashton of our plans. She is standing beside Ryder who has his arm curled protectively around her waist, looking like the cat who got the cream and Ashton looks concerned as she sees the state Sophia is in. "Are you ok, honey, do you want me to come with you?"

"It's fine, thank you, Ashton, I'm just, well…"

She looks around briefly and then fixes her eyes to the floor and Ashton looks at me with a nod of understanding. "Ok, I'll see you tomorrow, honey."

Sophia nods and smiles briefly before I almost carry her out of the room. As the door slams behind us she says in a small voice, "I'm so sorry, it's fine, you can go back, I'll just head back to my room."

"Like hell you will."

With a grim determination, I drag her behind me to my room. Seeing Sophia scared of just about everything is sending me insane and I can't turn a blind eye to it any more. This girl needs to tell me everything tonight because until she does, we don't stand a chance of setting her back on the right track.

CHAPTER 16

SOPHIA

That place scared the hell out of me. When Ashton met me, I thought I'd be fine. I even dressed for the occasion and fixed my hair and make-up as if I was going on a night out. The minute I stepped through those doors, I knew I'd made a huge mistake. It was like walking into Satan's lair. The noise alone hurt my ears and the men—well, they overpowered me. They were intense in not only their numbers but the sheer look of them. The women were no different. They were awesome and I couldn't stop staring. It was like a scene from a movie playing out right before my eyes. It was hot, sexy and a lot to deal with.

I tried to avoid the eyes of the men, but it was impossible to do. I felt a hunger directed at me that stole the breath from my body. It was as if I was for sale and they were deciding whether to buy or not. I'm not used to it. Men look away, or to the ground when I walk into a room. They avoid me like the plague because of who I am. These men don't care.

The women were scary in their own way because I couldn't even begin to compete with their beauty. Self-assured and confident, not afraid of anything and quick with the smart remarks. I felt so out of my depth; I was drowning.

Ashton took me to a corner away from the pack and I breathed a little easier. She ordered me a drink to settle my nerves and introduced me to two really friendly women who were good fun and interesting to listen to. Millie was serving the drinks and smiled at me sweetly, but I felt so bad for her and guilty that I had taken something she wanted.

I couldn't relax and when I saw Maverick, I just wanted to run to him but I was conflicted. He is one of them. He is part of this world and he plays as hard as the rest of them. It showed me a side to him I didn't want to see and I suppose I retreated into the hard shell I built around me to protect my heart from being trampled on. I couldn't look at him because I was full of disgust—for myself.

But when his hand closed around mine, it was a lifeline. I can't deny the feelings I have for him and so, here I am running after him, back to his room and by the look in his eyes, he wants answers and fast.

That alone is causing me to panic because the demons I live with will destroy me in a heartbeat if I let them out into the open. He will not be able to save me, no matter how much he wants to. He doesn't do mafia, he said, well; I *am* mafia and have to suffer everything that goes with the territory.

Almost as soon as we're inside his room, he points to the couch and says firmly, "Sit, I'll fetch you something for the shock."

On autopilot, I do as he says, trying hard to gather my shutters, ready to pull them down. I take a deep breath and count to ten because he cannot make me unlock that box I hide inside.

"Here, whiskey, it will give you courage to tell me everything I need to know."

"You think this is all it will take?"

I lift the glass to my lips and feel the liquid burn as he nods and sits beside me. "Yes."

"So, you want me to tell you something I can't even deal with myself when you won't let anyone in on your own secrets. As I said before—hypocrite."

To my surprise, he laughs softly. "Never pretended otherwise. But in your case, I'll make an exception."

"You will?" I say it in surprise and he nods, looking at me with a look that could melt an ice palace.

"Sophia, I don't want to fight with you. I want to know you. I want to understand what's hurting you so bad and I want to take that problem and make it mine. I'm stronger than you and can deal with it—for you. Let me help and then maybe you will understand and accept what I tell you about my own past."

"Why do I have to go first?"

"Because I have dealt with my demons and they are controlled. Yours are not and so you need to be in the right place before I unburden myself to you."

Once again, I raise the glass to my lips and take a deep gulp of the fiery liquid and feel the burn, then set it down and say with a determination I don't feel inside, "Ok, Maverick, you've got your wish but you should know there are consequences of opening Pandora's box."

"I can deal with that."

"Can you though? I'm not so sure, but well, here goes nothing."

CHAPTER 17

MAVERICK

At last, we're getting somewhere. Sophia is finally about to tell me what's scaring her so much and I'm eager to hear it.

I watch in fascination as she leans back and her expression changes before my eyes. She turns back to that mafia princess she wears so well. Her expression is blank and her eyes are dead. There is no feeling in them, just loneliness and resignation of a life that takes no prisoners.

"I told you what happened when I last saw Carlos Toledo. Well, he escaped and despite my brother's best efforts remained free. Then my brother heard he was in Chicago and headed straight there. It turned out it was an inside job and somebody that worked for us fed Tobias false information. I got the call to tell me to take Anastasia and he would send a car for us. To trust no one and keep his wife safe. The trouble is, the car that was waiting for us contained the very man himself and as soon as the door opened, I was pulled inside."

She stops and looks at me through tortured eyes. "When I saw him sitting there, it's as if everything played out in slow motion. Luckily, Anastasia was spared and the door closed behind me. I was so afraid, Maverick. I saw the madness in his eyes and knew I was in terrible trouble."

I try to remain composed but inside a fury is building that is hard to control. Then she sighs. "He hit me so hard my head hit the window and I must have blacked out because the next thing I knew, I woke up tied to a wall in a steel building. I wasn't alone."

She breaks off and for the first time since she started her tale, I see emotion in her face as she squeezes her eyes tightly shut and a tear escapes that she brushes angrily away. When she looks at me, I can see the torment in her expression as her breath hitches. "There was a woman tied to the wall with her arms above her head. She was almost dead, or so it seemed. She was naked and bruised and there was so much blood. It was a horror story that only got worse when I saw two children cowering on the ground in front of her, their eyes wide and frightened. They were also tied up and can only have been around 7 or 8. One was a boy and one a girl and the look they gave me will live with me to my dying day. They had so much fear in their eyes, I could taste it. I couldn't speak because there was a filthy rag binding my mouth and the ropes cut into my skin whenever I tried to move. My head hurt so much and yet I tried to stay strong for those children's sakes."

She looks at me with more strength and I know the memories are driving it because she hisses, "It turns out they were the family of the man who betrayed us. His wife and kids were held under the promise he would set them free when I was in his custody. The bastard never had any intention of it because he mocked us by telling us in graphic detail what he would do to them. The sick bastard raped the woman in front of us all and if the kids made a sound, he silenced them with a punch to the stomach. They were terrified and that poor woman was trying so hard to be strong and brave for their sakes. It seemed like hours later that he increased his perverted pleasure and turned his attention to the children. He stripped the girl and told us he was going to rape her in front of her mother and brother. She was crying and he held her down and I thought I was going to pass out I wanted to hurl so much. But the bastard just pulled out a needle and injected her with drugs. She was thrown against the wall like a rag doll and then he did the same to the boy, all the time taunting the mother and telling her how she would watch her kids die a slow painful death before he cut her up into pieces."

I feel sick to my stomach and I wasn't even there. It's no wonder Sophia is broken; anyone would be dealing with the horror she witnessed first-hand. I've dealt with shit in my life but never have I witnessed anything even close to this and instinctively reach out and pull her to my side.

She begins to shake in my arms and says fearfully, "At least the kids were asleep and the woman appeared to have passed out. I really thought she was dead, but it meant the space was filled with silence for the first time since I arrived and then he turned his attention to me."

Her voice breaks as she re-lives the horror and says fearfully, "He enjoyed tormenting me. He told me everything he was going to do to me in a hoarse whisper. He ran a knife up my leg and under my skirt and held it there. He told me he was going to rape me first and then do the same with the knife. He was going to let me live because there was a worse fate in store for me."

I watch as she closes down before my eyes by pulling back and turning away, so I pull her head to face me and say with a hard edge to my voice, "Tell me."

She blinks and I see the fear return as she falters and then says in a whisper. "He told me what was going to happen.

When my parents were slaughtered by him and his family, I thought that was the worst thing that could happen. When Tobias did the same to his, it was an eye for an eye. The rules we understand and live by. But Carlos told me of an approaching storm that involved me and my family that would make history repeat itself and I would lose everything I loved if I didn't agree."

"Agree to what?"

"To merge our family with another who was coming for us."

I can feel the pressure building as a white light goes off inside my head, as she whispers, "Someone was coming who was far more powerful than the Moretti's and Toledo's combined. They wanted it all and they were prepared to fight a dirty war. My only way of stopping it was to marry into that family and allow them to take over. Everyone knew that Tobias had never wanted to take his role at the head of the family. That was always Thomas's job, but when he was killed, Tobias had to step up. That made us weak, which meant they could destroy us all in no time if they wanted to. Carlos told me I was to be given to the head of that family in exchange for his freedom. He would pledge his allegiance to them and I would be imprisoned in a loveless marriage in a world I hate more than life itself. I had no say in the matter and if the family wouldn't agree to his terms, he would send me back to Tobias the same way he sent Thomas back to us."

Shaking her head, she pulls away and plays with her fingers nervously, before saying, "Then the Reapers stormed the building and the rest you know. The woman and children were set free and I was brought here. Carlos was handed to Tobias to dispose of and I was free to return with him. But how can I ever go there? There is a war approaching that will cost lives and tear my family apart. I'm the only one who can save us from certain death, but if I agree, I am sentencing myself to death by marriage. I just need time to work out how to play this because I can't tell Tobias because he would overreact and go in all guns blazing. What do I do, Maverick, because I could sure use some advice right now?"

I can feel my heart hardening with every word she speaks. Every shiver, every groan, every shaky word she says, pierces my heart. I have to know and yet fear the answer.

"What are their names?"

She turns away and I grab her face so hard she flinches under my hand. "I said, what are their names?"

I feel wild and out of control and think I know the answer before she says the word I fear the most.

"Romano."

CHAPTER 18

SOPHIA

The look on Maverick's face is scaring me. He looks so angry I should fear for my life right now. I've never seen fury like it and can almost taste the anger that surrounds him like a force-field. He stands and paces the room, curling and uncurling his fist, demonstrating that he is on the edge of losing control and for the first time since I met him, I feel frightened.

I don't speak because words are not what he needs right now. He is dealing with some serious shit and needs time. So, I sit silently, waiting for the storm to break that I brought to his door. I feel so guilty and wish I hadn't said anything, but how was I to know it would affect him this deeply?

He moves to the window and stares out into the darkness and my heart goes out to him. What is running through his head? It's difficult to say, so I wait.

Then he turns and the look he gives me makes me want to curl into a ball and hide forever. He has changed in an instant and I don't recognize the man.

He is cold, aloof and angry with a silent strength that

warns not to approach. I think I've done the wrong thing and then he says in a harsh voice, "We will deal with this."

"But how?"

I look at him in fear because, how can we? Can the Reapers really take on this war for us? I doubt it. Why would they?

Then Maverick changes again and comes and kneels before me, taking my hand in his and raising it to his lips.

His breath sears my skin and brands me his and as I look up, he growls and fists my hair and pulls me toward him. There's a frantic energy that drives us as we crash together like a ship on rocks. He tears at my clothes and I do the same to him because the only thing we want is to be naked. This is frantic, dirty love and is built on trust because anyone looking in right now would call the cops. The lamp goes flying as we crash into the table and the rug burns my skin as I scrape against it as he pushes me down and thrusts inside. I claw his back and fist his hair and swear I draw blood because his roar should scare me, but it drives me harder. He pushes inside me like a dirty beast and I love every minute of it. I just bared my soul to him and it wasn't enough. He wants all of me and I'm happy to invite him in. He owns me because I have been stripped bare in every way as he takes from me what no one has ever had.

Maverick claims me like a caveman and I love every minute of it. I scream his name as he pushes in harder, faster, deeper. He holds me down and the delicate skin on my arms puckers under his touch, but I don't care. I want him, all of him, and this is exactly what I'm getting. Dirty, rough sex, but so much more. It's a union of lost souls and as I clench his cock, he groans, "Come for me, baby because I can't hold on."

As I cum all over his cock, I scream his name and with a

roar, he pulls out and coats my breasts with every last delicious sticky drop of his release.

Then he wraps me in his arms and holds me tight and I feel his heart beating fast as our sweat glues us together. He holds me so tenderly but with an ownership that wraps me in protection and then he says huskily, "Pack your bags."

I pull away and feel the fear return. He's sending me away. How did I get this so wrong? He's sending me home to face this because there can be no other explanation.

Abruptly he pulls away and stands, walking around the room like an angry god in his naked glory. I feel so betrayed as he turns away and says in an emotionless voice. "I said go and pack your bags."

"But?"

I want to ask so many questions but he has shut down before my eyes. I trusted him and he is turning his back on me.

I don't know what to say and gather my clothes, feeling used, dirty and filthy. Did he mean to make me feel like a cheap whore? Is this because he has some grudge against the mafia? I don't do mafia, he said. Well, he just did and now I'm left out in the cold while he turns his back on me.

With a sob, I gather my clothes and run. I want to keep on running because how can I just pack my bags and leave? He can't make me, surely?

So, I run to my room and lock the door behind me. This can't be happening. What did happen? I thought we were on the same page, but the minute that name left my lips, he changed. What is he hiding?

∽

I SCRUB every inch of my body in the shower and it still won't remove the memory of his touch. I wash my hair and scrub my nails that raked his skin not thirty minutes ago. As I dress in the clothes I came in, I stare at myself in the mirror. Sophia Moretti, bitch from hell. Maybe I need to draw on that now because Maverick has betrayed me, I thought he was different.

A gentle knock on the door takes me by surprise and as I open it, I'm amazed to see Ashton looking at me sympathetically.

"I'm sorry, honey."

"Why, what's happening?"

She pushes her way in and pulls me in for a hug, rubbing circles on my back and saying softly, "I'll help you with your things."

"You're really sending me back?"

My voice is but a whisper because I can't believe it's come to this. She pulls back and shakes her head. "Of course, we're not sending you back. You're going to face your fear with a warrior beside you."

"What?"

I sit on the bed in disbelief and she takes the space beside me and squeezes my hand. "Maverick told Ryder you were leaving first thing in the morning. He is setting everything in place now. I'm to help you pack and make sure you get a good night's sleep because it's some trip you're heading on."

"Where are we going?" I almost don't want to know and I can't believe that Maverick is coming too.

Shaking her head, Ashton says with pity laced through her voice, "I don't know. They don't tell me the details, but wherever it is, it's resolving your situation."

"But Maverick, he was so angry. Why is he helping me?"

"Only he knows the answer to that. I know Ryder told me it's difficult for him. Whatever his problem, it's deep rooted and concerns the mafia. Ryder told me that he never gets involved with anything concerning the mafia but wouldn't say why. This will be hard for him, honey, so go a little easy and he'll tell you what you need to know when he's good and ready."

Now I feel even worse and she puts her arm around me and says reassuringly. "He's a good guy under that rough exterior. Trust him and you'll be fine. Do whatever he says because he will only have your best interests at heart."

"Will I come back?" I fear her answer because I'm not ready to face the outside world and this place is the only one I feel safe.

"I'm sure you will but it will be because you want to. Who knows where your journey is going to end but if it's right back here, then you can expect a welcome home party? If not, then I'll miss you. We all will but none more than Cassie and Caspian. I hope you do come back because I like having you around. We could be good friends and this place is not as scary as you think it is."

For a moment we just sit in silence as I try to process the turn of events. Where are we going? I have my suspicions and if it's what I fear, then god help me.

CHAPTER 19

MAVERICK

I haven't slept; I haven't eaten, and I haven't got the guts to tell Sophia where we're heading.

Romano. How that name makes the blood freeze in my veins. I knew it would be them. Fate's a bitch and has dealt me a low blow that I'm not sure what to do about. Do I tell Sophia and risk her walking away, or do I wing it and hope I can sort this without washing my dirty laundry in public?

As soon as she told me, it sent me wild. I fell on her like a savage beast because it was instinctive. I wanted to brand her as mine in a desperate attempt to keep her but how can I? She's right, this is bigger than both of us and I'm not sure I'll be able to save her this time. Am I prepared to unlock my own demons, to chase hers away? Do I love her that much? We've just met and yet it's as if we've always known we would arrive at this point. I have been running from this and thought I'd arrived at a safe place. I will never be free—of them and a past that haunts my future. Fuck me, I need a drink.

As I dress, I distract the bitter taste in my mouth by picturing Sophia. What must she be thinking? I was so cold for a reason. She will soon discover why I must be that way, but she will be hurt and disappointed in me. Maybe she should be. Maybe she should hate me for what I'm about to do. I hate myself and I hate where I'm heading.

As I look in the mirror, I shiver that runs deep inside. He's back. I don't do mafia, but that's a joke because the person staring back at me is mafia through and through. From the pulled slicked back hair, to the dark tailored suit. A black shirt with a black tie and the darkest shades in my pocket. To face the mafia, you have to be one and I hate every part of my body that welcomes this suit like an old friend. I don't do mafia because I *am* one.

Grabbing my bag, I take one last look in the mirror and set my mood.

As I walk to the courtyard where the car is waiting, I try not to think about what I'm leaving behind. Will I be back? I'll do my darndest to make it but nothing is certain when you dance with the devil. It's early for a reason. I don't want to answer awkward questions when the Reapers wake and see me dressed this way. Some of them know already, but some don't. The whores know nothing and that's just how I wanted it to remain. Maverick is a Reaper, created to escape a past that leaves a bitter taste on my tongue. I know Sophia because I walk in her footsteps.

As the driver stows my bag, I hear her approach, her heels clicking on the ground behind me. As I turn, she takes a step back as she sees me properly for the first time. She stares in disbelief at the black SUV waiting for us and I see the bitter realization that she will never be free flood her beautiful face. As she draws near, she stares at me with contempt and says in a cold voice, "You should have told me."

"Get in the car."

I'm cold and brutal because to know me she has to see me first hand. I open the door and she heads inside without a look in my direction and as the driver holds the other door open, I join her with a whole load of regret as a passenger. I can't look at the Rubicon as it disappears from view because it's where I'm going I need to concentrate on now.

It doesn't take long before Sophia asks the question I always knew was coming. "Who are you?"

"I'm your protector, your best friend, your lover and your worst nightmare rolled into one."

"That doesn't answer my question."

"Yes, it does."

She makes to speak but I place my finger over her lips and say in a cold voice.

"You asked me what I was hiding from. Your answer sits beside you. The only way you will ever truly understand, is if you see first-hand what that means. I will show you who I am, not tell you. I will prove to you that I was right to hide and you may not like what you discover. The one thing I can assure you is that I have your best interests at heart. I am not doing this for me, it's all for you, to set you free, at least I hope it is. What you need to understand is that there are no guarantees when you deal with the Romanos. You will see and hear things you will hate and will not pass comment on. You will do everything I tell you even if it tears at your soul and you will *not* question me. Do I make myself clear?"

She pulls away and nods, looking down at her hands and I hate the wall that has built up between us. I want to tear it down and tell her everything will be alright. I want to hold her in my arms and tell her I'll take care of her and nothing will ever harm her when she is by my side. But I can't. I can't make promises I can't keep, so it has to be this way—for now. She has to believe that I am ruthless, cold and calculating and she has to witness that first hand. In order to save an angel, I need to break her first and that will be the hardest part of all.

∼

THE JET IS STANDING by and as we draw up to the steps, I see the trappings of filthy money. A sleek silver jet with a black interior. It's always black. Black everything to reflect the dirt we deal with—hell, the dirt we are.

The stewardess waits at the bottom of the steps and smiles respectfully as we embark the aircraft. Sophia is silent beside me and that's a very good thing. We are not alone.

The usual guards have been sent to escort us and I don't miss the curious looks in our direction. They nod with a respect I've never understood and I ignore every last one of them. I'm cold and unapproachable for a very good reason and just take the whiskey the attendant hands me without passing a remark.

Sophia asks for a water and turns to look outside the window and I wonder what is going on inside that pretty little head.

As the jet taxis down the runway, I lean back and close my eyes, shutting the world out. I need this time to prepare myself mentally for a challenge that was always on the horizon.

CHAPTER 20

SOPHIA

This is my worst nightmare and I can't even speak. The emotion is tearing me up inside and I never saw this one coming. Who is this man beside me because he's not the man I gave myself to and enjoyed getting to know? This man is a stranger and from the looks of him, he's withdrawing from me as well as himself.

He's taking me to them—it's obvious. I didn't even get a say in the matter; he made my decision for me. Is he handing me over to set himself free from whatever hold they have over him? It certainly feels that way and now I'm right back where I started, in trouble.

Briefly, I wonder what Tobias would do if he could see me now. Flying straight to the enemy. The only hope I have is that Ashton thought it was a necessary step. She told me to trust Maverick, but how can I trust someone who has kept such an important piece of information to himself? Would I have come if he told me—I doubt it but now I'm here, I feel curious to see where this will lead. Am I to be married off to a rival family to prevent a war? Is this the only solution to a problem none of us wants?

Then there are the Romanos. I've heard of them, of course, but never took the time to really listen. Now I'm a fool because I'm going in blind. Whatever my fate is, it's a very different one to what I hoped for and yet the man sitting beside me is the only one I have ever fully trusted. Yes, I'm a fool because he has shut me out and I'm not sure if he will ever let me back in.

I look around and see the usual set up. Black clad guards that are all from the same mold. Courteous to a point, hiding a deadly heart. One false move and my life would be over—it feels as if it already is.

We don't speak for the entire journey, mainly because Maverick doesn't open his eyes. I know he's not sleeping, it's obvious, but he's shutting me out and I can only hope it's for a very good reason.

Three hours later, we touch down and I see a place that is unfamiliar to me. The sun is shining and has wide open spaces and leaning over, I whisper, "Where are we?"

"Florida."

I lean back and look with interest at a place Tobias never wanted to visit. I never really understood why, but the reason is probably all around me. The Romanos. They own this state and I'm guessing Tobias avoided it for that reason.

As the jet comes to a stop, the doors open and I sigh as I see the usual fleet of black cars waiting. Some things never change and so I follow Maverick to the door and without speaking, take my seat beside him in the second car. There are no words spoken and Maverick is keeping his cards close to his chest. The guards give nothing away and I wonder what hold they have over Maverick to send a jet and guards to bring him here. They obviously want him badly because this is quite something.

Once again, we don't speak and I guess it's because the walls have ears and I've lived in this world long enough to know that conversations are reported back. So, I sit beside Maverick and say nothing. There are no looks, no gestures and no indication that we even like each other, which makes me think he is delivering me straight to Satan himself.

It takes another forty minutes before we sweep through large electric gates into paradise. I thought I lived in a mansion, but this is something else. There must be acres of grounds, all manicured to the point of ugliness. Nothing out of place and so much wealth it leaves a bitter taste in my mouth. Drug money, extortion, and built on the bones of the damned. A beautiful paradise in Hell.

The cars sweep into a large drive set before the biggest mansion I think I have ever seen. Beautiful flowers decorate a white building that obscures the terror within its walls. Unlike my own home, this is modern and bang up to date, with huge pillars and modern lanterns with a composite driveway that must have cost hundreds of thousands of dollars to have made.

However, the most interesting thing of all about this house is the welcoming committee because standing waiting are three men. Unlike the guards, these men are dressed differently and there is no mistaking their power. Three men who exude a confidence that tells me immediately who they are because these men are not guards, but why they are waiting is what intrigues me the most. The Romanos.

Maverick is still beside me and I daren't even breathe. He is so tense I'm sure that one false move and he would shatter into a million pieces. There is so much tension in the air as the door opens and a guard says reverently, "Welcome home Mr Romano."

I stare at him in shock. What did he just call Maverick? This can't be happening. Before I can comment, Maverick exits the car and straightens up outside, before turning and offering me his hand.

Still, he says nothing and as he helps me from the car, the same man says, "Welcome, Miss. Moretti."

I nod and stare in shock at the faces of the men who wait. There is no mistaking them—all of them. The Romano brothers and Maverick is one of them.

I watch in disbelief as he heads toward them and I don't miss the interest in their eyes as he stops and says, "Brothers, it's been a long time."

One by one, they step forward and I shiver inside. It's too much power in one place because these men are the cruelest of gods. Devastating good looks, more money than the reserves and an edge to them that tells you one false move and you're dead.

I feel their interest and tremble inside. I stand like a lamb to the slaughter before three predators with capture in their sights.

One of them steps forward and says courteously, "Miss Moretti, we are honored to receive you in our home. You have obviously met Lorenzo, allow me to introduce the rest of the family. My name is Lucian and these are my brothers Romeo and Dante. We would like to welcome you to our home as a most welcome guest."

I feel their stares stripping me bare as I struggle to maintain a disinterested façade and just smile politely. "I am honored to be here."

Maverick turns to me and looks bored. "Maybe someone could show our guest to her quarters, we have a lot to discuss."

One of the brothers moves his head slightly and a woman comes hurrying out dressed in a maid's uniform and smiles warmly. "Welcome, Miss. Moretti, please follow me and I'll show you to your quarters."

Grateful to escape the obviously awkward homecoming, I don't even look back as I follow her inside.

CHAPTER 21

MAVERICK

I breathe a sigh of relief as Agatha takes Sophia inside because just her presence was setting me on edge. The fact my brothers were waiting told me everything I needed to know. This is not going to be easy and I need to maintain a cool head which I can't do when she is around.

Lucian nods and says in a low voice, "We should take this inside. You are right, business comes first."

As I follow my brothers inside a house I know only too well, I feel the walls dragging me back to a place I considered a prison for far too long. We head along the hallway to the den at the end of it. The usual place of business and as we walk, I can tell that nothing has changed. I left this place three years ago, almost to the day, and never thought I'd come back. The fact I'm here is a very big thing, which is why my brothers waited on the steps. Respect, that was the reason because they know only too well that one word is all it would take to rock their world and they will want to keep me sweet.

So, as we head inside the office and take our places, I ignore my usual seat and stand at the window overlooking the pool instead. I ignore the seat I was born to fill, preferring to stare at the freedom of the world outside this room.

They wait for me to speak and I turn and stare at them long and hard. If they are nervous, they make a good show of disguising it as they wait for me to speak.

"It has come to my attention that you have designs on the Moretti empire."

Lucian nods. "We are expanding, Lorenzo. Business is good and we need to capitalize on that. As you know, there are four of us and it's time to use our resources to expand. Word is, Tobias Moretti has lost interest and is strengthening his legitimate businesses over the family one. It would be foolish of us to allow another family to step in and take what could be ours, so we have decided to make them an offer."

Romeo laughs. "We just haven't decided which one of us gets the prize."

I glare at him with menace in my eyes and he looks interested. Dante shakes his head. "Enough, what we need to know is why you're back, Lorenzo? You walked out of here three years ago and turned your back on this family. You left us to pick up the pieces and now you arrive back with the woman we want the most. What's your plan?"

They all look to me and I shrug. "I don't have one. Sophia Moretti turned up at the place I live, running from this very problem. She refused to go back with her brother because Carlos Toledo told her the only way she could prevent a war between our families was to marry one of us. I thought it best to bring her here and settle it once and for all."

"And that's it, you really expect us to believe that?"

I stare at Romeo with a hard look and he throws it right back at me. Slowly, I move off the window I lean against and head toward him and say in a dark voice, "You got a problem with that?"

Dante jumps up. "Enough. We're family, we don't fight

among ourselves. He's got a point though, Lorenzo. What is this, are you ready to take your place, or have you not finished playing soldier yet?"

The mood is deteriorating fast and Lucian says roughly, "Enough. We've been in the same room for five minutes and we're already fighting. Now, we are brothers—family and that counts for everything. Miss. Moretti is our key to her brother and taking over where he no longer wants to be. She needs to marry the two families to prevent a war. It's up to each of us to persuade her it's in their best interests."

Dante shakes his head. "If Lorenzo agrees to return, he gets first choice, it's only fair as he's the eldest." He turns to me and says coolly, "This is your rightful place at the head of the family and the only way you can be considered is if you agree to take it. If you pass, it falls to Lucian as next in line to step up and marry the girl."

I feel as if I'm being slowly strangled to death. On the one hand, I have Sophia who I would die to protect but the price is one I am unwilling to pay. Will I sacrifice my freedom to save her? I knew this was coming and I brought her here, anyway.

My brothers look at me awaiting my answer and I feel as if I can't breathe. Fucking mafia, how I hate that word and everything it stands for. If I marry Sophia, they drag me back to a place I hate with a passion. If I don't, I lose her to my brother.

Hobson's choice. Whatever happens, I lose.

A knock on the door interrupts our meeting and Lucian says tersely, "What is it?"

The door opens and the woman, who glides into the room, has us all to our feet in an instant. She looks at me and the tears in her eyes bring a lump to my throat as I whisper, "Nonna."

She moves toward me, her arms outstretched and as I

wrap mine around her, she cries in my arms. "Lorenzo, mio angelo."

"It's good to see you, Nonna."

As I hold my grandmother in my arms, my heart beats a little faster. She's the one remaining part of our past left and the only person alive who would dare interrupt us. She has always been there, a light in a raging storm. She has seen and suffered so much and of everyone here, she is the one I have missed so hard it hurts.

"Come, Lorenzo, I want to look at you."

She pulls back and looks me up and down critically and shakes her head. "Too thin. You need to eat more, mio angelo."

My brothers roll their eyes because I could be obese and she would still want to fatten me up. It's what she does, care for us, and I've missed her cooking so much.

"Come my angel, I will cook for you. You can see your brothers later at dinner."

Thankful for the easy escape, I follow her outside and she winks as the door closes behind her. "There, now you can breathe, no?"

I laugh softly because she's a wiley one and I know that whole performance was to get me out of an awkward situation.

As we walk, she holds onto my arm and whispers, "It's good to see you, Lorenzo. I have missed you, we all have. Now, tell me about the Moretti girl. Is she pretty, does she look as if she could provide an heir? Does she have good manners and is she feisty?"

Laughing, I stop and hug her hard. "Oh, how I've missed you, Nonna."

Her eyes soften and she says softly, "You may not believe me but we have *all* missed you, Lorenzo. When you left, you unsettled the throne of power. Lucian is a hard man, much more ruthless than you ever were. He lacks your balance and makes a good warrior but is no diplomat."

Thinking of my younger brother, I have to agree. He was always the one most fond of battle. Hard, cruel and merciless. He would think nothing of ending a man's life, even if there was another way. Of all of us, he is feared the most and I hate the fact he controls the empire that should rightfully be mine.

"What about Romeo, is he still fooling around?"

"You know him, what do they call it, oh yes, still a player? More interested in the women and what they can offer him, than settling down with a nice girl and giving me a reason to stick around."

I laugh as her eyes soften and she says, "Dante has missed you. He has been lost and struggled to find his place. He tries but I know he is lost ever since…"

She breaks off and I squeeze her hand. "Still no word."

"No, they keep on looking but she has disappeared from earth itself. He can't move on until he knows what happened."

Thinking about my younger brother, I feel a sharp pain in my heart. Dante is the most serious of my brothers and his feelings run deep. A few years back, he fell in love with his childhood sweetheart. She got pregnant and he made plans to marry her. Then one day she was gone and nobody knew where. He looked everywhere, but there was no sign. It was as if she disappeared off the face of the earth and he has never stopped looking. My one regret was that I left him to live with his pain alongside my two unfeeling brothers. He would have struggled and I was so intent on saving myself, I turned my back on him.

We stop outside the kitchen and nonna smiles. "Now, go and fetch your friend, I want to look at her and make my own mind up. You will find her in the yellow room."

It's only when I'm halfway there, that it strikes me I've been set up. Nonna could have sent one of the maids to fetch Sophia, but she has given me the opportunity to spend some time with her without anyone else around. As I quicken my pace, I hope to God she'll let me in.

CHAPTER 22

SOPHIA

Lorenzo Romano, fucking liar. I am so angry I almost can't breathe. He knew. He always knew who I was and the minute I told him my secret, he was no better than Carlos and fucked me and then rejected me. I thought I knew him; it turns out I did. Will I ever meet someone who loves me for the girl I am and not the position I sit reluctantly in? It doesn't appear I will because it's proved to me one thing—I am never safe. Even in a place I thought they could never touch me.

For a moment I consider calling Tobias. I would feel like such a fool. I should have gone with him that night. I should have told him immediately about the war coming and allowed him to prepare the troops. Why did I think I could make it all better? I'm nobody. The typical mafia princess who is used in another way by her family. Marriage. To another family—a worse family than my own because the Romanos are way more to deal with than the Moretti's. Four times more fear, four times more pain and four times more of a problem and *he* is one of them.

I don't unpack. The kind maid showed me to a very

pretty room decorated in yellow. It is welcoming and the sunlight that bathes the room lights up any shadows and brings warmth to a cold prison. But I'm not staying—how can I? I will not be delivered to the enemy as a willing guest. I need to make a stand and show that I'm not going to play by their rules—but how can I without leaving the same way my brother did when he was returned home to us?

A gentle knock distracts me and my heart starts beating fast—it begins.

I watch the handle turn with a morbid curiosity. Who will they send?

As the door inches open, I look away as I see Maverick enter the room and look at me with a tortured expression.

I don't want to know.

I feel him approach the bed where I sit on the edge, straight backed and unfeeling, and feel it sag as he sits beside me and takes my hand in his. Quickly, I snatch it away and move to the window, turning my back on him and trying to blank him from my mind—he has other ideas.

Moving behind me, he crowds my personal space and grips my waist, drawing me back into his body and it strikes me how well we fit. But then again, I know we are the perfect fit, or at least I thought we were.

Leaning down, he whispers, "I told you to trust me, you must hold that thought above all others. I warned you what to expect and by the end of this, you will hate me and rightly so."

Spinning around, I make to slap him hard across the face and he catches my hand and his eyes glitter with a danger he keeps well hidden.

I hiss, "Trust you, how can I? I don't know you."

"You do know me, Sophia. You have always known me. I was always coming for you; we both know that and now we are in an impossible situation. War between our families unless you agree to unite us by marriage. It should be so easy, but it is the cruellest of choices."

"Why?"

I stare at him with hurt in my eyes and he groans, pulling me roughly to him and holding me with a possession that makes my head reel and my heart pant. "Because if I do the right thing by you, I lose myself. Do you think it was easy for me to walk away from this - my family? Do you think they made it easy on me because you know how valued family is? My decision was one that took a lot of thought and a lot of guts. I never wanted this; you should know more than most what that involves because your own brother has also made that decision. I have three other brothers who are willing to step into my shoes. They thrive on this life and so business never suffered. If anything, I handed the reins to a brutal successor who loves nothing more than ruling this kingdom with no mercy and no shit. Now I'm back because of you and we have a decision to make. Stop a war by marriage, or start something that will not end well on both sides."

I push him away and say angrily, "Then leave, go back to the Reapers and carry on with your day. You've brought me here and your job is done. You can hurry back to the place you hide in and forget about the world you have delivered me to. But I'll tell you one thing for free, I would rather die than marry one of those men and if that's what it takes, I hope it's quick because what sort of life would I have if I agreed to the deal? Married to an unfeeling bastard as a business arrangement. Well, newsflash, I don't care about living because what does that mean, anyway? This life isn't living, it's a slow painful death that tortures your soul before delivering you to an afterlife where it happens all over again. So, fuck off whatever your name is, your job is done."

I turn away and close my eyes against the bitter tears that

threaten to reveal how wounded I am. He can't see that part of me, I won't let him.

He has other ideas.

Suddenly, I am crushed against him and he fists my hair and holds my head in place as he kisses me so ferociously it takes me by surprise. There is so much passion behind this kiss. It knocks the breath from my lungs like a powerful punch. He grips me hard and presses me against him and I have nowhere else to go but him. My traitorous body responds like the whore it is, and I kiss him back with a passion that makes a mockery of everything I've just said. Then he pulls away and stares at me, his eyes flashing with a possession that makes my blood run cold and yet tells me I have nothing to worry about.

He is not finished with me yet.

He leans down and whispers, "Now shut the fuck up and do what I tell you because I'm going nowhere. You will fucking trust me because all of this is for you. I will not turn my back on you and if it means sacrificing my soul, I would do it in a heartbeat. There *will* be a way out of this, I just need time to figure out what that is, so put up and shut up and play the game because there is more at stake than your wounded pride. Now, come with me, there's someone I would like you to meet."

Grabbing my hand, he pulls me from the room and my head struggles to keep up as we almost fly down the corridor to God only knows where.

I don't have time to register my surroundings because Maverick is on a mission of his own and I'm along for the ride.

My heart thumps inside me as I wonder who it is and I hope to God it's not one of his brothers because they scare the hell out of me. It's too much breathing the same air that is laced with so much intent and I need a moment to settle my nerves but it appears I'm not allowed even that.

However, I stare in surprise as we head into a large kitchen and the woman that looks up as we enter takes my breath away. If I thought those men had power, it is nothing compared to hers because as soon as I lay eyes on the majestic woman looking at me with interest—I am lost.

CHAPTER 23

SOPHIA

"Miss. Moretti, come in and take a seat."

Her voice is kind with an authority that warns you to do as she says immediately.

She turns to Maverick and smiles warmly. "Mio angelo, you may leave us."

He hesitates and she laughs, her eyes lighting up with an understanding that she obviously enjoys because she turns and looks at me a little differently.

"I said leave. You will see, Miss. Moretti at dinner along with your brothers. You should change and take the time to settle back into your old room."

He looks at me with a thousand apologies in his eyes and I turn away pointedly, making the woman laugh even more.

I hear the door close behind him and then feel her hand in mine and turn to look at her in surprise.

"Welcome, Sophia, I am sorry your visit is under these circumstances."

I try to smile but it's hard and she shakes her head sadly. "You must be worried, my dear, but you have no reason to be. Lorenzo is a good man and will find a way."

"A way out of what?"

"Your predicament. We are both women who know only too well what it is like living in a family such as ours. My grandsons are difficult, complex men and are no different to my husband and son."

I look at her with interest and she smiles. "Allow me to fill in the details. My name is Elena Romano. My husband, Vittorio was the head of the family the entire time I knew him. Like you, I came from a rival family and our marriage was arranged against my will."

I make to speak and she silences me with a look. "History does have a habit of repeating itself over and over again and this, my darling, is the sad truth of the world we live in. I was the lucky one. Vittorio was a jewel among trash. He made me feel like a queen for our whole life together and yet I was under no illusions he had a dual personality. With me he was loving, kind and everything a girl could wish for. He respected me and made my life as easy as possible living under these circumstances. We loved each other with a passion that surprised me given the circumstances of our union. When Georgio was born, I was happier than I ever thought possible. Then along came Sara and Francesca."

I am riveted to her story because she is giving me an insight into a world that sounds so different to mine. It almost appears normal and how can I not be impressed by that?

Then her face clouds and she sighs. "My children were much like you, unwilling to accept who they were. The girls did everything in their power to turn their back on this life and had a hard time because of it. You see, a normal life is not an option when you fear you may not be around long to live it. We have many enemies and need the guards to keep us safe. Georgio met Maria, the boy's mother, and she was not from this world. It was not a successful marriage because she struggled to understand this life we live. It ate at her soul and when Dante was just five years old, she took her own life."

I stare at her in horror and she shakes her head sadly. "Those poor boys were left without a mother and I tried to step into her shoes. So, you see Sophia, those boys are like my own and like any mother, I excuse their flaws and celebrate their strengths. I see them in a very different way to you and wanted to reassure you that they are not the demons you think they are. I know the reason for your visit and I sympathize but you really have nothing to worry about."

"Don't I?"

My voice is hard, which I regret because she is being so kind and she laughs softly. "I hoped you were strong because that is a quality you will need more than anything. Strength and love."

"You think I have that option—love?"

Her eyes sparkle with a light that settles my heart - a little. "I see love in your future, my darling. You see, like all mothers, I know my children more than they know themselves. When Lorenzo left the family, he broke all our hearts. We have never stopped hoping for his safe return, which is why this is more important than you will ever know. Failure is not an option because you, my dear, are the glue that will bind this family together and I think you already know that."

"Me? I am nothing. Just a way for your family to get richer and control an even bigger empire. Why should I be any different to any other daughter of a family that has something they want?"

"Because you give me hope, Sophia. Your situation reminds me of my own all those years ago and the one who brought you here is struggling to stay. He is battling his own feelings because he wants to turn his back and walk away, but he can't."

"I'm sure it won't be long."

"You're wrong."

"How do you know? We've been back here for five minutes, he's changed."

She smiles sweetly and laughs. "Because the way he looked at you when he brought you to me is the same way his grandfather used to look at me. You're wrong, Sophia. Lorenzo is going nowhere without you by his side, which is why I need you to trust him and go along with the plan. If you do, you might just save you both and get the future you both want, just don't do anything foolish and trust in God to deliver you on the right path."

Leaning back, I think for a moment and then smile.

"They are lucky to have you, Mrs. Romano."

"Call me Elena, my dear. I am your greatest ally here but also your worst enemy if you upset my boys."

She stares at me with a fierceness that makes me smile. For all her sweetness and soft approach, this woman is harder than all the men here. A shell that has built over time and many years of hard living and I'm guessing she has endured so many horrors I couldn't sleep at night Yet she has survived and well by the looks of things and all because of the love of the right man for her.

"Tell me about your husband, Vittorio."

Her eyes dance as she laughs happily. "He was a bastard. A ruthless bastard who drove me to distraction in every way possible. I could be angry with him one minute to the point of driving a dagger through his heart and then forgiving him in an instant when he smiled and lit the flame inside my soul. He was everything to me, Sophia, and when he died, it was as if a part of my soul died with him."

I almost don't want to know but say sadly, "How did he die?"

"Cancer."

I wasn't expecting that and she shrugs. "He was the lucky

one. Nature extinguished his flame when it could have been much worse. All the money in the world doesn't buy your health and if mother nature decides your time is up, there is no bargaining with her."

"I'm sorry."

I smile with sympathy and she shakes her head. "Don't be, we had many happy years and he was aging fast. It was his time and at least he had Georgio to hand the business to. You see, Sophia, Georgio was like Lucian. He thrived on this life. He married Maria because he wanted her and when a Romano man wants something, they take it without having to work too hard to get it. But Georgio lacked the love in his heart that his father had. He didn't treat Maria the same way I was treated and lacked the patience to understand she was struggling. He started to look outside the home for entertainment and became cold and cruel. It was too much for such a beautiful creature who craved the light and she overdosed one night when he was away."

"How old was Lorenzo?"

I can't imagine the pain he must have gone through and she sighs. "He was ten years old. The boys are close in age and had each other at least but I'm not sure if they have ever really come to terms with her death and each deal with it in their own way. Lorenzo blamed the life we live for destroying her, which is why he felt the need to run. Lucian is like his father and god help any woman he marries because I can see history repeating itself there. Romeo chooses to forget inside every woman he meets and Dante has a sadness to him that only increased when he lost the second woman he loved, which makes him more deadly than the lot of them. So, you see, Sophia, they are all struggling and the only thing that has remained constant in their lives is the family business. This is what keeps them going and so don't take it personally when you think on the reason you are here."

"Why are you telling me this?"

"Because it's something you need to know. I'm guessing you are scared, hurt and confused and rightly so. Don't get me wrong, these men will break your family to protect their own which is why you need to put your faith in Lorenzo because he is the only one who can save you."

She looks up at the clock on the wall and stands quickly. "Look at the time, I have rambled on too long. I will have one of the maids show you back to your room so you can dress for dinner. We eat as a family and there is never business brought to the table. Take the time to understand those boys and look behind their cold eyes and ruthless attitude. They are just the same as your brothers and if anyone knows what lies behind the blackest heart, it's a woman that's lived this life."

Almost as soon as the last word leaves her lips, a maid different to the one before appears and I wonder if there is some sort of hidden summoning device I don't know about. The maid curtseys as if she is in the presence of a queen and Elena says kindly, "Emma, please show Miss. Moretti to her room and help her if necessary. Dinner will be served in one hour."

She then turns to me and I see a flash of steel enter her eyes as she says firmly, "Think on what I have said, my dear. It was said with good reason and only a fool would disregard it. Don't be a fool because I'm counting on you to be better than that."

I nod and whisper my thanks before following Emma from the room. For all her sweetness, Elena is the most ruthless one here. I can see that because that little speech was in itself the starkest warning. I have no choice—this is how it is and I can only hope that the man I marry is the one they want the most—Maverick.

CHAPTER 24

MAVERICK

Just being here is crushing me. The air is always different here. Denser, choking and laced with threats and tension. I'm not sure why I thought bringing Sophia here was a good idea. Maybe we should have remained at the Rubicon and hidden away until my brothers grew tired of searching? Then again, I'm a fool if I thought that was ever gonna happen.

As I dress for dinner, I hate the fact I have slipped back into my role here as if I've never been away. The clothes I wear caress my skin like an old friend and remind me of how easy it is to live with great riches. As Maverick, I live a more basic life that is one hundred times better than this. There I have no responsibilities other than doing my job when I'm required. Ridding the streets of the very people my brothers do business with, which is why my one rule was that I don't do mafia. I may have turned my back on being one, but I will not betray my own kind on the instructions of a government who are more corrupt than any Mafia Don.

I almost consider calling for Sophia to escort her down to the meal, but I know that would show my weakness in an instant. So, instead, I allow the maid assigned to her to show her the way and head down to join my brothers in the den for the usual pre-dinner drink, where we discuss business before leaving it behind to enjoy a family meal.

Dante is the only one there and he looks up and nods as I step foot inside the room.

"Lorenzo."

"Dante."

As I fix myself a drink, he says thoughtfully, "What made you return?"

"I thought that was obvious."

"The girl?"

"Her name is Sophia."

"Of course."

His voice is laced with humor and it irritates me. "Have you got something to say to me, Dante?"

"Rather a lot as it happens but I doubt you want to hear any of it."

"You're right."

He sighs and then lowers his voice. "When you left, Lucian took it upon himself to prove that he was more than capable of filling your shoes. You should be worried about that."

"Why, he's welcome to it?"

"Because of the family name, reputation and respect our father built up."

"You think they respected our father? He was no different to Lucian. He was a tyrant that had no feeling and I blame him for ruining all our lives. If Lucian decides to model himself on a monster, that's up to him."

"Keep on telling yourself that, Lorenzo, only you believe you mean every word. Tell me, if he marries the girl, would it bother you?"

I consider my answer carefully because Dante is no fool

and it's obvious he's seen something I'm not willing to reveal. "Should it?"

"If you love her it would change everything."

"Love." I almost spit the word. "Love gets you nowhere, Dante, of everyone you should know that. Where has love ever got any of us? Love has ruined your life and you have never stopped searching for something that probably isn't there anymore."

Immediately he reacts and flies at me and I face him down like the soldier I am. Getting in his face, I fix him with a look of warning he would do well to heed because I have always been the strongest brother and he obviously remembers that because he snarls, "You know nothing about me brother, you chose to walk away—remember. If you think love has destroyed me, then you are more lost than I realized."

"Well, isn't this nice?"

We look up as Romeo heads inside the room straight for the whiskey bottle. "Brothers scrapping like the kids they still are. Don't expect me to join in, I grew up years ago."

He regards us coolly and I shrug and turn away. Dante also retreats, and Romeo laughs softly. "You know, I almost envy your choice, Lorenzo. Miss. Moretti is an intoxicating woman. She would look good on the arm of any man and I'm guessing would be quite the whore when required."

I push down the anger his words were designed to create and just shrug. "From what I've heard, you'd know a lot about whores, brother. What's the matter, can't you interest a real woman long enough to stick around?"

He just laughs and raises his glass. "Touché. No, my problem is getting them to leave. What can I say, I'm a good catch?"

"That's a matter of opinion."

Lucian heads into the room and looks at me warily. "Have you made your decision yet?"

"No."

He sighs and reaches for the same bottle my brother has just replaced. "Well, don't take long about it. If I am to marry Miss. Moretti, I don't want to waste any more time. If you decide against it, I want your written confirmation that you won't come back and challenge me for my position. This ends now, Lorenzo because it's too unsettling for the guards, our associates and this family. We need clear lines to operate within and if I'm to step up and take charge on a permanent basis, I want to do so with no blurred lines."

He stares at me with the intense look that I know so well. My father looked at us in the same way and the steel behind his eyes reminds me of that man and how cruel he could be. Maybe Lucian is the perfect successor because he has a thirst for this life where I had my fill years ago. I already know I want no part in it but to throw Sophia to a monster is not my style and leaves a bitter taste in my mouth, so I say in a dark voice. "Then I am prepared to negotiate."

Immediately, I have their attention and Lucian says in a low voice, "We're listening."

"I have no interest in picking up where I left off and am happy for Lucian to take charge, on one condition."

I see the spark of interest in Lucian's eyes as he leans forward. "Name it."

"You walk away from the Moretti's and set Sophia free."

I think I hold my breath because I expect I've played right into their hands. They will now know I have feelings for her because I shouldn't care what happens to her but it's now obvious, I do.

Lucian says slowly, "Interesting. So, you would give all this up for a woman."

"That's not what I said."

Romeo laughs. "It sounded like that to me."

"Then you haven't understood, I see some things never change."

Romeo makes to rise and Lucian snaps, "Sit down."

He turns to me and says in an emotionless voice. "Why would we do that, it doesn't make good business sense? The whole purpose of marrying the Moretti girl is to expand our empire in a place we don't control. Her brother is weak because he is looking for a way out and if Miss. Moretti becomes a Romano, then we have access to their network. We could easily take that over in exchange for a cut, keeping her brother in the style he is accustomed to. If we let her walk away, we would lose access to all that and nothing would change. This isn't an emotional one, brother, it's business and that, as you know, comes above everything."

I turn away because I thought as much. It was never about Sophia and they are not interested in bringing me back into the fold because it compromises their own positions.

Romeo laughs softly. "If we agree and let the girl leave with you, what would that achieve? Lucian's right. Nothing would change, so how is that good for business?"

"What about her brother?"

Dante raises the subject nobody has mentioned until now, and Lucian shrugs. "I'm guessing if his sister is ok with it, he would be too. Once we've agreed a course of action, then she will contact her brother and tell him the happy news. We would set up a meeting and assure him of our best intentions and offer our management services, enabling him to concentrate on his businesses that he appears to value higher than the family one. Everyone is happy and Lorenzo gets his freedom."

"Do you really think that brother—that everyone will be happy?"

"If you're talking about the girl, I can assure you I will make her *very* happy."

My brothers laugh and it's like pouring acid on my heart picturing Sophia married to this unfeeling bastard. It would destroy her and yet if I stepped up, I would never leave a place that destroys my soul.

Dante stands and sets his glass down. "We've run out of time. Nonna will be expecting us. My advice would be to settle this tonight and then we can move on. There are two choices. Lorenzo stays and marries the girl, or walks away and Lucian takes his place. The decision is yours, Lorenzo, you have until the morning to decide."

He makes toward the door and we stare at him in surprise. I wonder when he became so cold. Of all my brothers, he was always the one to sit in the background and let the rest of us fight among ourselves. He had no interest in the business or forming an opinion, yet now he appears to be the coldest of us all.

Lucian watches him go and then says in a low voice. "He's changed, Lorenzo. There is no hope left and he has switched off from life. The perfect mind set for the job we do, but we all know that isn't the real him. He will self-destruct and we will be left to pick up the pieces. Talk to him and see if you can get through to him, unless you intend on leaving in the morning that is."

He stands and nods toward the door. "We must go, we can't keep the women waiting."

As we follow him from the room, I feel the walls closing in on me. I've been here for five minutes and I already feel trapped. This is an impossible situation and I don't know what the hell to do about it.

CHAPTER 25

SOPHIA

As meals go, this one feels like the last supper. I am sitting dressed in a long red dress that clings to my body like a well-fitting glove. Apparently, they had a whole new wardrobe delivered for my visit, which totally took my breath away. I had everything I could wish for waiting inside a walk-in closet that would rival any high-end store. This family certainly know their stuff because the whole pretty woman thing is intoxicating.

I am now surrounded by four delicious devils and one incredibly powerful woman, eating food that wouldn't look out of place in a top restaurant, served by liveried servants who are silent and blend into the shadows.

It's a world away from life at my own home with just Mrs. Billings for company and if I wasn't so scared, I would find this whole set up spell binding.

Maverick is seated beside Elena who is at the head of the table at the opposite end to me. I feel it was deliberate due to the daggers he is throwing his brother Lucian as he refills my wine glass. I am seated to his left and beside me is Romeo with Dante opposite him. Maverick sits beside him with Elena at his side at the opposite end to Lucian.

Feeling the scrutiny of every person here is a lot to deal with and makes my glass reach my lips much more than it should.

The food is divine and the conversation stilted. There is an undercurrent of tension that Elena is trying hard to diffuse.

My hand shakes a little as Lucian fills it once again and he leans across and whispers in a low, deep voice, "Relax, Sophia. Nobody here wishes you harm."

I stare into the darkest eyes I have ever seen and swallow hard. "Are you sure about that?"

He looks at me with interest and then laughs as he sees Maverick looking at him with a frown.

"It appears that my brother has an issue with me, I wonder what that could be?"

I shrug and steal a look at the man himself and shiver inside. I can tell he is on the edge and one false move could turn this civilized meal into a full-blown war and as our eyes connect, I shiver for a different reason entirely. That look is promising me that he hasn't even got started with me yet and makes thinking about anything other than him very difficult. However, Lucian has other ideas and leans close, whispering, "My brother has a decision to make that he's struggling with."

I stare at him in surprise, "Which is?"

"You."

"Me?"

He laughs softly. "You see, Sophia, my brother likes to keep his cards very close to his chest. He is a private man who lets no one in. The fact he delivered you to me tells me he has allegiance to this family that he can't just switch off. He knew we were always going to find you and for reasons of his own, he chose to deliver you personally. That tells me he has an interest in you because he has made it crystal clear he has no interest in us, our grandmother aside. So, you are the reason he is here, which is of great concern to me."

"Why do you care?"

I take another gulp of my wine and he says darkly, "Because I have no desire to see him back where he belongs almost as much as he does. However, unlike him, I put the family business first and am prepared to do whatever it takes to make us invincible. Lorenzo gave all that up when he left and if he returned, it would be unwillingly."

My head spins as I look at Maverick and see the unhappiness on his face. He is tortured and I know it's because of me. He doesn't want to be here—I know that and yet he came, anyway.

Lucian whispers, "If he chooses to marry you, he will be sucked back into this life. If he walks away, he leaves you behind to face it alone with me by your side."

I stare at him with fear and he laughs softly. "Make no mistake, I would make your life more comfortable than you could ever imagine. You would want for nothing because as my wife, you would control all you survey. All I would ask is your share in your family business in return for bearing my children. We would have a union of business with many delicious benefits. I'm not offering you my heart, Sophia, but I am offering a good life in exchange for your loyalty. If Lorenzo chooses to stay, that would be a problem for me and for you."

"Me? How is that a problem for me?"

"Because he would hate every minute of it."

"Excuse me."

He laughs and I watch his eyes flash with a ruthless spark that makes my blood run cold. "He thinks he wants you now but when the passion settles, it would leave a bitter taste in his mouth. He would begin to resent the fact he gave up his freedom for you and after a time, begin to hold you responsible. You would always know you had been the ruin of him and your perfect love would shatter and die. You see, Sophia, the biggest act of love there is, is sacrifice. If you love my brother, you will set him free—us all free to follow the path our hearts desire. You may find I'm not so bad after all and realize that you made the correct choice in the end. Think about it because you are the only person here who has that power."

He turns away, leaving me shattered. As I steal a look at Maverick, I am not surprised to find him staring at me with a yearning I most definitely understand. My heart fills with so much love because I see the lost man inside of him who is trying to do the right thing and can't see a way out of this situation. Will he give it all up for me and come back to a place he doesn't want to be? I already know my answer to that as we share a look that promises a path set with passion and destruction. Yes, Lucian is right about that—the decision will be mine to make because do I love Maverick enough to set him free and lock the door behind him to live in a gold-lined prison with a bastard?

I think I always knew the answer to that.

CHAPTER 26

MAVERICK

The second I saw Sophia sitting beside my brother, I knew. I have no other choice. I am coming home with her as my wife. There is really no other choice because she is mine and it's taken coming here to make me realize that.

I watch him whisper his poison in her ear and know there is nothing I can do to stop it. Whoever organized this seating plan knew what they were doing because it has made my mind up in a heartbeat.

"She's a beautiful woman, Lorenzo."

Nonna leans in and whispers, and I smile. "She is like you."

"You flatter me, mio angelo, but then you always were a charmer, just like your grandfather."

She smiles and says sadly, "I miss him so much. He always knew what to do, even in the most difficult circumstances. I wonder what he would make of all this."

Feeling the guilt she is shoveling on me, weighing me down as she intended, I shrug it off. "He would understand."

"Are you sure about that, you see, family was everything to him, why is it so hard for you?"

There is no answer to that because family *is* everything to me, just not this one. I have a new family now and it's tearing me apart that I may not have a choice to return home, so I shake my head and says gruffly. "I will do the right thing."

"For you, or for her?"

"Both."

She leans a little closer and whispers, "Don't let infatuation rule your heart, Lorenzo. You have known this girl five minutes and she is not your problem to solve. Lucian would make a good husband, but we both know there is more to it than that. When I fell in love with your grandfather, it was not immediate, you know that. I grew to love him and she could do the same."

"Or he could destroy her like my father did my mother."

"He could, there is always that option."

Once again, I look at Sophia and my heart twists inside me. She looks so beautiful, but I can tell she's afraid. She sits there like a cornered animal, her great beauty dazzling like a star trapped in a darkened room. She deserves better than this—better than me because I am weak and she doesn't need that quality in her life right now. Maybe nonna is right and I should walk away for my own self-preservation. But that would also destroy me, so I know my decision before the main course is even served. I will marry Sophia to save us both and figure out the details at a later date.

My attention turns to Dante who is sitting beside me locked in his own little world.

"Tell me how it really is with you."

"I told you, I'm fine."

"Have you met anyone since…"

He laughs dully. "Yes brother, I have met many women

since Ava, just none of them measure up. It doesn't mean that I don't use them to satisfy an ache inside me that never really goes away."

"Are you sure you've left no stone left unturned?"

"Do you take me for a fool, Lorenzo?"

"Of course not."

"Then don't treat me like one. If Ava was anywhere, I would have found her by now, so I must face the fact she's probably dead. I must move on and let go and try not to remember what love felt like."

He pushes his plate away and growls, "Have you made your decision yet?"

"I have."

He looks at me with interest. "Which is?"

"You'll know soon enough."

He laughs and I see a little of the light that used to be part of him return as he smiles. "Then I will look forward to the fireworks."

Romeo is now talking to Sophia and she looks as uncomfortable as fuck. God only knows what line he is spinning her, probably one to get her in his bed. It strikes me that I don't trust a single one of my brothers that sit around this table and yet I have fifty more back at home who I would trust with my life. That's a real family. One that chooses to be one, rather than the one fate thrusts upon you. Once again it makes my choice an extremely difficult one, but the woman who drives it deserves the best even at my own expense.

By the time the meal is over and we retire to the living room, my nerves are so ragged I almost can't see straight. I need some time with Sophia on our own to lay out my plan and I pray to God she accepts my offer.

Sophia sits beside nonna and my brothers take the surrounding chairs. I prefer to stand by the window and the atmosphere is awkward as fuck. We are all skirting around the real issue here and I can tell Sophia is on edge, which is nothing to where I'm hanging right now, so after a while, I snap. "Sophia, can I have a minute?"

She looks up in surprise and I don't miss the smile that passes across the face of my grandmother and the razor-sharp stare of Lucian as Sophia blushes prettily and excuses herself. Watching her walk toward me, reinforces my decision because I have never seen her looking so beautiful as the flush to her cheeks and the brightness of her eyes betrays her feelings.

I nod toward the open door and say nothing as she follows me outside. Once we reach the peaceful garden a cool breeze causes her to shiver and I place my jacket around her shoulders and say huskily, "Follow me."

I don't take her hand and I don't speak until we are some way from the house obscured by trees. I know that won't mean anything because every meter of this place is guarded by cameras, but I know a way around that and duck into an alcove near the citrus trees and pull her into my arms.

She jumps back a little and I hold on tight and say firmly, "Now listen to me."

She nods and I can't resist the temptation of Eve as I tilt her head back and kiss those lips that beg for it. She moans against me and I pull her tight and growl, "You're mine, nobody else's, they will have to deal with that."

"But how? This is an impossible situation?"

Stroking her hair, I hold her tightly against me and whisper, "This is not how I imagined it to be. I want the best for you and I want to give you the world. It's only been a short time but long enough for me to know I can't let you walk away. Something about you is deep inside me and I know if I lost you, my life would be meaningless. So, with that in mind and despite the reason we are here…"

I pull back and stare at her with an intensity that makes her color a little and then I drop to my knee and take her hand, saying simply, "Sophia Moretti, will you marry me?"

CHAPTER 27

SOPHIA

I stare at Maverick in total shock. I can't believe he just did that. He is kneeling before me promising me the world—everything I want and I should be ecstatic. But how can I be? This is a forced proposal because we have run out of options. This is a deal to be made for business rather than love. I am under no illusions that he is doing this for me and my world comes crashing down at the realization I have only one answer possible.

"No."

He blinks in disbelief and shakes his head. "No?"

Taking a deep breath, I say with a tremble to my voice. "I can't marry you, Maverick."

"But why?"

"Because this isn't the answer. You are doing this out of some misguided sense of what's right for me but if it meant you had to give up everything you worked so hard to build, of course my answer is no."

He nods with an acceptance that tears at my heartstrings. He's giving up without a fight. I did the right thing.

I fully expect him to leave but instead he pulls me close and drops a kiss on top of my head and says roughly, "It's ok, I understand. We'll find another way."

For a moment, I cling to him, wishing like hell things were different. We may have only just met, but I feel as if I have known him forever. If time allowed it, we could fall in love at leisure and allow fate to direct our future. This is all contrived, rushed and the product of panic and I know I have done the right thing—for him, anyway.

The silence is oppressive because it has created a wedge between us and then he surprises me again by pulling back and kissing me so gently it makes my soul shiver. He traces my lips with his thumb and his dark eyes glitter with intent as he says gruffly. "Stay with me tonight."

I nod because I want that more than anything. Being without him is like living without a heart—impossible.

I almost can't ask but say fearfully, "What happens next?"

"We stall for time while I try and figure a way to take you back with me."

"Will they allow that?"

"I'd like to see them fucking try and force my hand. No, darlin', if marriage with me is not on the table, it doesn't happen—period."

Feeling relieved, I raise a smile. "You're a little sure of yourself, aren't you?"

He nods and his eyes flash. "We both know I am. Make no mistake, if I wanted to, I could have you married to me within the hour. Nothing you could say could change that because we both know the world we live in. As the head of this family, my word is law and I'm almost tempted to force your hand."

"You're a little arrogant, aren't you? What if I genuinely don't want to marry you, have you even considered that?"

"No."

He smiles and I sink against him with relief and whisper, "Ask me again six months from now when we jog in the forest surrounding the Rubicon. Then you can ask me again when you cook me breakfast and serve it to me in bed with nothing but a promise in your sexy dark eyes. That's the sort of proposal I want from you, not a rushed knee jerk attempt to keep what you think you own. I want the world Maverick and I kind of think only you can deliver it."

Once again, we kiss—a seal on an agreement that both of us want to honor. The trouble is, it may be out of our hands.

We reluctantly head back and I feel the interest of the family watching us approach. I can tell they are expecting some kind of resolution, but I take my seat beside Elena and smile. "It's a little chilly out there."

She smiles slightly and looks at Maverick with a thoughtful expression and he just raises his glass to her and knocks back the brandy in one. If I see a little disappointment in her eyes, it is quickly replaced by a loud yawn. "Well, the perils of getting old I'm afraid. I need to retire to bed and leave you all to gossip about me when I've gone."

She winks as Romeo offers her his arm and we bid her goodnight as she is helped sweetly from the room.

It feels a little awkward as Maverick nods toward me. "Ready?"

Lucian laughs darkly. "So, you've made your decision."

I feel my breath hold of its own accord as the room turns silent and Maverick shrugs. "Sophia is my woman, Lucian and we will not be bullied into something that neither of us want. You will just have to think of another reason to make me stay, or is the point of this that you want me to never return? Either way I'm done with your threats and for the record, the Moretti deal is blown. There will be no alliance and no marriage. If it comes to it, you will start a war with more than Tobias Moretti. You see, you forget that I have contacts with every mafia family in the country and if it came to it, I would use them to stop you getting your hands on something that belongs to me."

Lucian jumps up and I stifle a scream as he advances menacingly toward Maverick, backed up by his brother Dante. I can feel his rage in the air, it's a tangible force that promises the deadliest revenge. It's all too much as Lucian snarls, "So you would turn your back on your own blood to save another family, treachery at its most stupid. I never had you down as a fool, brother, you know how this will end."

Maverick stands his ground and immediately I see my future before me. A deadly war with casualties on every side. Family against family all in the name of love and I will not be responsible for that. Standing quickly, I say loudly. "Enough."

The men stop and look at me and I say in a cold voice. "There will be no war, not because of me. I will not be the catalyst that forces destruction. I don't want to marry any of you. I want to be free of this fucked up life and live among normal people. If it comes to it, I would rather take my own life than be witness to any more bloodshed, so you can all go to fucking hell."

Without even looking in their direction, I storm from the room intent on getting out of here as quickly as possible. I'm not sure if that's an option but I need to try at least and there is only one man who can help me, god help him.

Somehow, I make my way back to my room and slam the door. I drag a chair across and prop it under the handle and try to take a few deep breaths. With shaking fingers, I do what I should have done in the first place and type out a text that I never wanted to send.

As I press 'send' I try not to imagine the problems that text will bring the one person who is ignorant to his life being bargained in this way. My brother has the right to an opinion, so I send for the cavalry and wait for the battle to commence.

CHAPTER 28

MAVERICK

I am so angry. At myself, my brothers and Sophia. More than any of that, I am upset that Sophia walked out. As soon as she left, I pushed past my brothers and headed for my room. She needs to cool down, but I will not give up on her without a fight.

As I take the time to cool down myself, I realize how stupid my statement was. Of course, I wouldn't go against my family. It was a bluff that was called and now I'm back where I started. I'm in unknown territory because more than anything, I want to wrap Sophia in my arms and get the hell out of here back to the Reapers and a life I know I need to survive. If anything, this has reinforced the fact this isn't what I want, but *she* is.

I must try and think of a resolution to our problem for close on two hours before it becomes impossible to continue. I need to see her so badly it's a physical ache and so I head across the hallway and knock tentatively on her door. There is no answer so I try the handle and find it won't budge and realize she has barricaded herself in—clever girl.

However, this house does not allow its guests such luxury,

so I walk into the next room and try the door that leads into the walk-in closet in her room. I don't feel bad about invading her privacy because I know she will be scared and confused and will need reassurance that everything will be alright.

The room is in darkness as I head inside and I listen for any signs of life. A soft whimper causes the blood to rush to my head as I feel my way to the bed. As I slip under the covers she stirs and says with fear in her voice, "Maverick?"

"Hush, darlin', it's me. You have nothing to fear."

She sighs and settles into my arms and says sleepily, "You're a little overdressed, aren't you?"

I need no further invitation and shrug out of my clothes and pull her warm, soft body against mine. A low moan escapes her lips as she whispers, "I need you so much."

I capture her words on my lips and taste my future. We share a sweet loving kiss that promises love, not lust. She shivers against me and I run my hands across her body and pull her in tight, groaning, "I need you, baby."

She pulls me close and whispers with an urgency that mirrors my own. "Fuck me, Maverick, make it count."

I need no further invitation and with a feral growl, crush her lips to mine in a bruising penetrating kiss and growl, "You're mine, Sophia, you always will be."

She reaches down and strokes my cock with a pressure that drives me crazy and I slip my fingers between her swollen pussy and stroke her clit, causing her to gasp and moan with pleasure. I can feel her arousal coating my fingers and lift it to my lips and lick them clean, causing the beast inside me to roar. She wraps her legs around my waist and moans, "Fuck me so hard I can feel you forever."

I don't even stop to think and thrust inside like the beast I am, pounding and searing her delicate flesh with my heat. She moans as I build a rhythm she matches with ease and she clings onto me hard, digging her nails into my back as if fearing to fall. The darkness mixed with the heat from her body sends me over the edge and as my balls slap against her ass it sends me to the edge of oblivion. Then I pull back and she groans in disappointment and I push her down and growl, "Not yet."

I kiss and bite my way down her body until I reach the place I've just entered so hard and fast. This time I taste it for myself and love the way her sweet juices sit on my tongue, tasting like the purest nectar. As I bite and suck, she bucks against me and moans with pleasure. Her hands dig into my hair and pull it hard and I love the fight in her as I eat her alive.

I can feel that she is ready, so I flip her over and pin her down and growl, "I want every last delicious part of you."

She whimpers as I pull her hips up to face me and spread her thighs, smearing her own juices on her ass. Then I hold my cock at the opening that invites me so crudely and gently ease the tip in, plunging my fingers into her pussy and hooking them against her g spot. As I stroke, I thrust and as I reach the promised land, she pushes back against me and screams my name as I cum hard inside her ass. She convulses against me as the waves of her orgasm rip all the fight out of her and she collapses against me, impaled on me like a virgin sacrifice.

I hold her against me and kiss her sweet neck, whispering over and again that I love her. I'm not afraid to show her the emotion in me because she needs to know that I do love her more than anything and to allow me to make this sacrifice in the name of it. Sophia has to marry me for the world to keep on spinning. If she doesn't, I may as well quit it, anyway. What price is it to pay to hold on to something so right against a life that is so wrong? We can make it work; we have to.

The night is ours and we don't waste a moment. I make love to Sophia every hour of it until she is sore and bruised and marked inside and out. I'm like a wild animal claiming its territory and she is a willing participant. It's as if this is our last chance to make it count and sleep is the furthest thing from my mind.

By the time the dawn arrives we are exhausted and reluctantly I leave her to grab a few hours' sleep and head back to my room, hoping that her mind is now aligned with mine. Today will be our wedding day because I'm in no doubt now, Sophia Moretti will become a Romano to save her family and the only one that will be is me.

CHAPTER 29

SOPHIA

When I wake, I feel the evidence of last night on every part of me that counts. I am bruised, sore and aching but wouldn't change a thing. It feels as if I'm a marked woman and I love every delicious bit of it.

I manage to drag myself to the shower and love the way the hot jets soothe the burn and wash my pain away.

Everything has changed because my mind was made up the moment Maverick entered my bed.

A gentle knock at the door reminds me I wedged it closed and I grab a towel and shout, "Just a minute."

Hoping to God it's Maverick, I am slightly stunned to see who has come calling.

"Elena!"

She laughs as she sees me dripping, shielded by nothing than a towel and says softly, "May I come in, my dear?"

"Of course, please."

I hold open the door and she glides into the room and sits on the bed like a queen visiting a subject.

"I trust you slept well, my dear."

I blush and the knowing sparkle in her eyes makes me wonder if we were a little loud and my face burns as I remember the sex marathon that went on here last night.

She looks at me with a considered expression and says gently. "I'm sorry, Sophia."

"For what?"

"For dragging you here and putting you through hell."

I just stare at her in surprise and she smiles ruefully. "I think you should get dressed and pack your bag. We are going on a little trip."

My heart twists as I wonder what the woman before me has up her sleeve and I say fearfully, "With Mav...um Lorenzo?"

"Not this time. It's probably best if we keep this between ourselves."

She sits and stares as if waiting patiently for me to do as she says and I notice she is dressed as if to go outside. Feeling concerned, I race to the bathroom and chuck the few possessions I brought with me into my bag and quickly change into the clothes I came here in, tying my hair in a messy ponytail rather than keep her waiting longer than I need to.

Wondering what this is, I try to find out as we walk through the quiet hallway toward the front door. I'm almost afraid to ask and whisper, "Where is everyone?"

"They had a meeting to attend and will be gone for two hours. Plenty of time to put this situation right."

I feel increasingly nervous as I follow her and there's something so final about it, my heart twists in my chest. I have to know and say fearfully, "Does Mav... um Lorenzo know?"

"No."

Now I'm really worried and almost back out but there is something about the way Elena looks at me that tells me she is doing me a huge favor here, so I follow her silently to a large black car that is waiting outside.

One of the guards holds it open and as we settle into our seats, steps into the passenger seat beside the driver. Then we set off with another car in front and one behind and I realize this has always been my life and probably always will be. As we pass through the streets, I picture life with the Reapers and how free I felt. Everybody looked after themselves and yet if you needed extra help, there were many willing hands. That is living as far as I'm concerned, not this charmless existence in a strange and deadly world.

Elena sits silently beside me and it's only as we stop outside a hotel in town, that she places her hand on mine and says sweetly, "Please forgive me, Sophia. One thing you should know before you leave."

"I'm leaving, what you're not coming inside?"

"No, my angel, my journey carries on but yours ends here. I just want to say one thing. When Lorenzo called and told us your story, we were surprised."

"What about?"

"That you thought you were to be married off to one of my grandsons in return for your business."

My mouth drops to the floor and I whisper, "It was a lie?"

She nods. "Carlos Toledo was obviously playing with your mind because we are not animals, Sophia, we conduct our business in a much more civilized way."

"But…"

I can't think straight as Elena laughs. "Lucian was the one who thought we could use this to our advantage. He wanted to provoke Lorenzo to declare him the rightful successor and renounce any claim he has to the throne of pain, as they call it. We all knew Lorenzo would do anything to walk away and Lucian thought this was a good way of tying up the loose ends. To see where his heart really lay and finalize things once and for all."

I almost can't form the words and say, "Does Maverick, I mean, Lorenzo know?"

"Of course not. I think he surprised himself by his reaction to it all and I knew he would do anything to keep you by his side. That is why I am intervening and setting you free. When Lorenzo turned on us all last night, it was obvious he was never going to be the head of the family we need. His heart just isn't in it and so we abandoned our plan and have decided to let him follow his heart. You must also do the same because it's obvious you are not cut out for this either. Lucian will head up the family and Lorenzo will return to where he is happiest."

"But can't I go with him?"

"That's why I'm sorry, my dear. Lorenzo has always been a man who prefers to live alone. He has many women as I'm sure you must accept and has never really shown any interest in keeping one. The life he now lives suits him because from what I understand, there are no strings attached and he needs this time to discover the man outside the mafia. Set him free, Sophia, because he is in unchartered territory. This will have destroyed him and you need to allow him to heal. If you are truly meant to be together, then you will find a way, but you need to discover who Sophia Moretti is first. So, your future is not ours to arrange. I am delivering you back to your own family and you must discuss it with them."

"My family!"

My heart lurches as the door opens and I see a familiar face looking at me with respect. "Miss. Moretti."

"Matteo."

He nods and offers me his hand. "I've come to take you home, ma'am."

I accept his outstretched hand as if in a trance and don't even register that I've left the car until it speeds off before I can even say goodbye.

As the guards crowd around me in front and behind, I am swallowed up into the familiar and ushered inside.

CHAPTER 30

MAVERICK

I can tell she's gone the moment I step foot inside the house. It's as if the life has left the building and now I know why I just endured a wild goose chase across town for my grandma.

My brothers had business to attend to and nonna asked me to collect a letter from her attorney because she had nobody else she could trust. As I step foot inside the house, she is waiting with a hard glint in her eye.

"Lorenzo, follow me."

I do as she says because we learned early on that the real power behind the throne lay at the hands of this woman and my heart sinks with every step taken.

She leads me to her office, a pretty room overlooking the garden, and points to the seat in front of her desk.

"Sit, we have much to discuss."

I do as she says because she will have the answers I need and look at her expectantly as she fixes me with a disapproving look.

"We have decided that you are no longer required to take

your place at the head of this family. You are free to return to your new life, on one condition."

I just stare at her in shock because I was not expecting this. She leans forward and says in a hard voice. "You will return for one weekend every month to visit. You will not sever ties with us because we are your family whether you like it or not."

A cold feeling grips me as I fear the worst and say harshly, "And Sophia?"

"Has been returned to her family. There will be no arrangement and no marriage, the deal is off the table."

I almost can't register what she's saying and say angrily, "What do you mean she's gone, where?"

"Calm down, Lorenzo, remember who you are talking to. Now, this is how it will be. Lucian has agreed to step up and lead the family with Romeo and Dante as his joint seconds in command. You will always be a part of this family, but not in the business. Sophia has been returned to her brother because their business is no longer any concern of ours."

She leans back and I see the ruthless glint in the eye of a woman who always puts her family first. "You have what you wanted, now go and pack your bags, you leave immediately."

"Not until you tell me where Sophia is."

"I've told you, back with her family where she belongs. You see, Lorenzo, you were two of a kind. Both unhappy with the lives fate dealt them and looking to escape. You found yourselves thrust together and sought comfort in one another's arms. You cannot build a future on that, so we are giving you both time to readjust to the situation. Sophia is safe and free to decide her own future and so are you. You both have what you want, Lucian has what he wants and I'm working on the other two."

She smiles so sweetly it's in direct contrast to the woman who just told me to leave and I'm surprised to see a tear edge down the crease in the corner of her eye as she says softly, "If yours is true love, then it will bring you back to each other. Distance will create meaning and if you are meant to be together, you will be. I always wanted the best for you; you must believe that. If you are happy, I am happy and being here was not the answer. You need to find the man inside you before you can care for a woman. This is our final offer and is non-negotiable. If you sign the papers that release you from the family business, you can only return as an inactive family member. It's your choice but know you are always welcome here, which is why I must insist you visit."

She takes the envelope that I retrieved from her attorney and pushes a sheaf of papers across the desk and holds out a pen. "Sign your life away, Lorenzo, and go and find a new one. Just make sure that you're happy because if you find it's not what you thought it would be, there is no going back."

It's strange, but as my grandmother offers me my freedom, it leaves an empty feeling in my heart. This is it; I've won. I'm finally free—then why does it feel so empty?

She smiles with a sadness that tells me how hard this was for her and as I take the pen, I almost feel her willing me to snap it in half. But I don't. I sign my name on the dotted line for the last time. Lorenzo Romano and stand up to leave as Maverick.

As I kiss my grandmother goodbye, I take a moment to relish my victory, but it's a hollow one. I'm leaving my home as one person, but that means shit when I leave alone.

As the black car drives me to the airport, I call Sophia for the entire journey. There is no answer and I must leave a thousand messages. Then, just before the car pulls up to the aircraft, I make a different call.

"Maverick, was your mission a success?"

"Not entirely, I need a favor."

"Name it."

"Sophia has been returned to her family; I need to know where that is."

"It will take a while, where are you?"

"On my way home. I'll call you when we're close, if you could arrange transport?"

"Of course. Consider it done."

As I cut the call, I feel the anxiety tear me apart. What did my grandmother tell Sophia? Knowing her, it could be anything and that's what worries me. If Sophia thinks I sent her away, then she will never take my calls. I need to find her and fast because my grandmother was wrong about one thing. I don't need time to work out my feelings for Sophia Moretti, I did that when I met her jogging through the forest. It's just taken this to drive the message home. I can't lose her now, not when I've finally got my freedom. Now I need to arrange her own freedom and that will be the toughest mission of all.

CHAPTER 31

SOPHIA

I feel like such a fool. In less than five minutes I am to be returned to my brother and he will be so angry. I've let him down; I know I have. By not choosing to leave with him, I've brought another family into our business and made him look weak. He also had to interrupt his honeymoon, which was his one shot at letting go of this tainted business by leaving it in the hands of his second in command—Matteo.

We are currently on a boat heading for the Hideaway. The Island my brother bought that, as its name suggests, is well hidden in the Pacific Ocean. The only way here is by boat and with charts that only my family have access to. Nobody will ever find me here and it should have always been the place I ran to. Not the Reapers. Not Maverick. Then again, the pain slices through my heart as I think about what I've left behind. *Him*. My one shot at a normal life with a man who sets my pulse racing and my heart fluttering.

As the shoreline comes into view, I swallow hard as I see I have a welcoming committee of one man. Tobias Moretti. Mafia Don and a man with no heart. My brother.

Blinking back the tears that sit behind the black shades that hide my pain, I prepare to meet him for the first time since before I was taken. He watches us approach with an impassive expression that he wears so well and I wonder what the outcome will be of this meeting.

As the boat docks at the side of the jetty, one of the guards jumps out and secures the rope and Matteo turns and lends me his hand as he prepares to hand me over to another.

As my foot touches the jetty, I prepare myself for the showdown I expect, but as it turns out what happens next takes me completely by surprise.

Stepping forward, Tobias pulls me toward him in his iron embrace and hold me so tightly I think I may break. I can feel his emotion as he whispers, "Thank God."

The tears now have no hope of staying hidden as I sag against him and sob as if my heart is broken. This is exactly what I needed because for so long I have held it together but there is no need for that now - I'm home.

By the time we pull back, the guards are gone and it's just the two of us alone on the jetty. Tobias looks completely different to the man I left and I can tell that marriage agrees with him. He looks tanned, healthy and content and I stare at him in wonder. "You look good, Tobias."

"I wish I could say the same."

His eyes narrow and I lower my eyes, which obviously irritates him because he says firmly, "Look at me, Sophia."

I raise my eyes and he frowns. "The only thing that matters is you're home. We can discuss the details later, but now you must settle in and get some rest."

He half turns and I feel the walls closing in on me already, even though we are standing out in the open in a tropical paradise. "Tobias."

I say his name with a softness that makes him turn and I say with fear, "What happens next?"

"What do you want to happen, Sophia?"

"Do I have a choice?"

He appears almost irritated and snaps, "Of course you have a choice, I'm not a monster, I'm your brother—family. Why do you look at me as if I am?"

Because you are.

The words remain unspoken but I know he hears them because he nods with a resignation that takes me by surprise. Beckoning me across to a bench that sits overlooking the ocean, he says softly, "I suppose I've never given you reason to think otherwise. However, I thought you knew. You are my right hand, Sophia, my blood, my conscience and my responsibility. You are the only one I have left of a family that suffered the cruellest of deaths. You are everything to me and I would die to keep you safe. What I want for you most is to be happy and I doubt you have found that yet."

"You're wrong."

He raises his eyes and stares at me thoughtfully. "I have found happiness, Tobias. I found it in the strangest of ways. It crept upon me when I wasn't looking and turned what should have been my darkest hour into my brightest."

"Then why are you here?"

A simple sentence that takes me by surprise. "Because I was sent here by the family, we fear the most. They had no further use for me and delivered me back to you. As it turns out, nothing was how it seemed and now I'm left to deal with the pain of betrayal."

His eyes narrow. "The Romanos?"

"I'm not sure."

He appears exasperated and sighs heavily. "Tell me the facts, Sophia and I will judge them on that."

By the time I finish my story, he looks even angrier than before and spits, "They treated you like a fool, a pawn in their own family games. I have one question though, why did you think marrying into that family gave them access to our business, that's what I don't understand?"

I almost fear his reaction when I say in a whisper, "They see you as a man who wants to walk away from this life and that makes you weak—in their eyes. They believe that it's only a matter of time before another family takes what you don't want by whatever means possible. They saw this marriage as a means of providing you with the protection you need should that ever happen and by offering you a way out of the business. They would manage it for a cut and it would be because I was married to the head of the Romano family."

Far from looking angry, Tobias just nods with a thoughtful expression. "I see."

Then he says harshly, "And this man, Maverick, do you have feelings for him?"

I look down. "I do but I'm not sure he feels the same."

"Why not?"

"Because he is much like you. He doesn't want this life and by marrying me, he would have been dragged right back into it. He was prepared to do that for me but he would have resented it and when the shine wore off, probably regretted his decision."

Tobias just stares at me with the cold hard look I remember so well. Then he holds out his hand and says firmly, "It is probably for the best. Families belong together and any man that turns his back on his, is not to be trusted. You deserve better, Sophia, you always did."

As I take his hand, I can't agree. He didn't see the torture in Maverick's eyes when he made his decision. He was prepared to give up everything for me and that is why Elena was right to intervene. I hope that he's happy now, back with the Reapers where he belongs. I try not to picture Millie comforting him and expect he will soon put all of this behind him and move on with someone else. I may not be so lucky, but at least I have my memories of a time that I actually lived to keep me warm at night. Nothing can take them away from me, they are all I have left.

CHAPTER 32

MAVERICK

It's been three weeks and still no word. Sophia's phone has been disconnected and the only intelligence we have is that she remains on her brother's island. Coming home should have been the sweetest of homecomings, but it just felt empty because she isn't here. Everyone expected me to pick up and carry on, business as usual but, how could I? I left the most important part of me back in Florida and I will not rest until I get it back.

"Penny for them, honey?"

Millie hands me a beer as I sit brooding at the bar and I frown. "Nothing to tell."

She almost hesitates and then leans forward and whispers, "You miss her, don't you?"

I say nothing but take a swig of my beer and set it down as she reaches across and takes my hand.

"Maybe you should go and get her, Maverick."

I raise my eyes and look at her with curiosity. I can see she hates telling me to go and get another girl when she wants to take her place, which softens my heart toward the pretty woman I have spent many a night with.

"Easier said than done."

"Easier on who? You're a Reaper, Maverick, not a quitter. If you want something badly enough, you go and do your best to make it right. Use everything you have to find her and convince her to come back with you, only then will you find peace."

She blinks back the tears and I look at her in a different light. Such a pretty girl who is longing to find her happily ever after. Part of me wishes I could have given her that but fate had other ideas and made my own happiness something I need to work hard to get. I squeeze her hand gently, whispering, "You're a good woman, Millie. You deal with things the right way and will make some lucky guy very happy one day."

"Just not you." She smiles sadly and I look at her with an apology that is long overdue. "I wish it could be but for some reason my heart went in a different direction. You're right, though."

She looks surprised and I push the beer away and give her a rare smile. "I'm a Reaper and we never give up. Maybe it's time I acted like one."

She smiles and her whole face lights up and then we hear someone calling her name, effectively switching her attention to another Reaper someway down the bar. She smiles ruefully. "Duty calls. I'll look forward to seeing you both when you return."

She heads off and I watch one of the guys reach across and whisper something in her ear that makes her laugh. Yes, Millie will be just fine because they always are—here, anyway. One day she will get her happily ever after and now it's time to fetch mine home.

As it turns out, I must wait another week because Ryder told me the Moretti's are due to visit Antigua in two days' time. Sophia is continuing to stay with her brother and his new wife on their extended honeymoon while their house is re-built and their boat, the Island Star, is reported to be docking in The English Harbour the day after tomorrow. Ryder arranged my ticket and so I am checked in and waiting for them to arrive. I am not alone.

As I relax by the hotel pool, a shadow stands in front of the sun and I look up and groan inside. "What are you doing here?"

"I could ask you the same thing, brother but we both already know the answer to that."

Lucian sits on the sun lounger next to me and snaps his fingers at a passing waiter. "Bourbon, on the rocks and whatever my brother is having."

"Water." I shake my head and laugh softly, "What's this, the pressure driving you to drink?"

Lucian settles back on his bed and smirks. "You'd love that, wouldn't you? Well, as it happens, I'm here on business, unlike you who is probably here on a fool's errand."

"You think?"

"I know because what you don't know is that I have been busy in your absence."

I try not to let it show but an uneasy feeling creeps over me at the smug look on his face and I say with a yawn. "I'm happy for you."

"I doubt it, you see, I am here to meet Tobias Moretti to strike a business deal."

"Is that so? Then we are on the same page because I too am here to strike a deal with that family of my own."

Lucian laughs. "Then may the best man win."

I give nothing away because this is unexpected. Seeing Lucian here raises the temperature and I wonder what he has planned. For a while we just sit in silence and I notice the carefully placed guards around the pool, trying to look inconspicuous but failing miserably.

After a while, I say gruffly, "How are things with the family?"

"Since you left, as normal. You see, Lorenzo, nobody was surprised when you signed your freedom papers. We all knew your heart was lost to this family years ago. If anything, it makes us stronger because now we have someone running things with no distractions and a thirst for the job at hand. But nonna is not happy with that and is keen to move things on, which is why I'm here."

"And the reason is…"

"Providing an heir, of course, what does grandmother always want?"

As quick as a flash, I am on my feet and my brother joins me. We are as close as can be without touching and I sense the protection moving in fast. I'm not a fool and they will be under instructions to shoot to kill and so I hold my ground and snarl. "That better not involve Sophia."

Lucian just smiles in his usual evil way and shrugs. "I'm not at liberty to discuss business with you, Lorenzo. Like I said, you made your choice and there's no going back. Now, if you'll excuse me, I should change because if I'm right, they will be arriving within the hour."

He turns and I have no choice but to let him leave. This time, anyway.

If my brother has designs on my woman, then he can expect a war because I am not leaving without her by my side.

CHAPTER 33

SOPHIA

"You look beautiful, Sophia, that color really suits you."

Ana sits beside me looking amazing in a black dress that hugs her curves in all the right places. The diamonds that glitter at her throat and wrists reflect in her eyes and her blonde hair is piled high on top of her head, framing those beautiful blue eyes.

Spending time with the newlyweds has been a bitter pill to swallow. On the one hand, it makes my heart burst as I see how happy she makes Tobias. I never thought I would ever see the side to him that she brings out and I want what they have. They are so happy and it strikes a need inside me for the same. However, it also makes me miss Maverick even more and I wonder if things had turned out differently, we would be in their position now. I like to think so because there hasn't been a minute that passes that I don't think of him and wonder what he's doing now. Absence has made my heart much fonder and I wonder if I will ever stop hoping for the impossible dream. There has been no word from him at all and I check my phone religiously. So many times, I have drafted a text only to delete it at once. Nonna's words ring in my ears as she told me to give him space to discover the man outside the mafia. I need to give him that at least and just pray he comes back to me.

However, as the weeks pass, my hopes begin to fade as it becomes obvious he must have decided it was no longer worth the trouble and has gone back to his old ways.

That hurts the most and as Ana lays a sympathetic hand on my arm, she smiles, "It will all work out in the end. I'm a great believer in that."

We share a smile because for the past three weeks I have unburdened my soul to Ana. While Tobias worked, we sat chatting and sunning ourselves on the Island Star as we cruised around the Caribbean. I told Ana about every minute of my time with Maverick, even the dirty parts, which we giggled over like schoolkids and kept as our little secret from a man who would hit the roof if he ever found out.

Now we are waiting to meet the man I fear because he has a proposition for us. Tobias told me that Lucian Romano will be joining us for dinner as they discuss business. There was a spark in Tobias's eye as he studied my reaction and I felt the fear return. I know that look. Tobias has been plotting behind my back and I have an uneasy feeling about that.

We make our way to the upper deck where Lucian Romano is due to meet us and I watch as Ana walks over to Tobias and his hand slips around her waist and pulls her gently to his side. He leans down and brushes her lips with his and that one soft gesture makes my heart twist with pain. Love. Such a powerful emotion and one that has changed my brother forever. Who wouldn't want that and it makes it even harder because I had it for the briefest of moments?

Then we hear footsteps and I spin my glass in my hand nervously as I see Lucian Romano heading toward us looking dark, dangerous and devilish in a black dinner suit with a black silk shirt. His eyes are covered in the blackest of shade and his hair is cut short and makes him look even more menacing, if that's possible. Tobias greets him and introduces him to Ana and I watch as he kisses her hand gallantly and then he turns to me and I feel the full force of his gaze as it enters my soul and strips it bare. He approaches me and lifts my hand to his lips, saying politely, "Sophia, you look beautiful."

I smile and pull my hand away quickly, which doesn't go unnoticed and his eyes glitter dangerously making me shiver inside.

Tobias clicks his fingers and the waiter approaches with a silver tray laden with champagne and we help ourselves and take our seats around an impressive dining table set up on the deck like the finest dining there is.

Ana looks at me sympathetically as I struggle to breathe. Her look is one of pity and I steel myself for what is coming. Surely, he wouldn't - I thought Tobias was better than this.

As we eat, the conversation is of everything but business and Lucian appears relaxed in our company, despite being on a rival family's yacht. I wonder why he's here and have no appetite for any of the delicious food served to us because it turns to dust in my mouth as I await my fate.

Only when the brandy and cigars come out, does the air change and Ana start to look worried. Tobias looks at me with a thoughtful expression and then says loudly. "Lucian, we have business to discuss that won't wait another minute. Have you brought the contracts?"

Lucian snaps his fingers and one of his men races over and thrusts an envelope in his hands. I think I hold my breath as he removes the papers and hands them to Tobias, who reads through them thoughtfully. We all sit like frozen ice sculptures as we wait for him to absorb the words and then he nods. "It all appears fine. I'll have my lawyer check them over and sign and return them to you one week from today."

Lucian appears pleased and says darkly, "And your end of the bargain?"

I feel them all stare at me and say roughly, "This had better not concern me."

I narrow my eyes and Lucian looks at Tobias and nods. Tobias says in an even tone. "We will let Lucian explain."

I feel them all watching me and struggle to breathe as Lucian says darkly, "I have struck a business deal with your brother for a share in your family business."

I stare at Tobias in shock and he nods. "Our conversation got me thinking, Sophia and I began to see the sense of it. I contacted Lucian and we agreed on a mutually beneficial deal. As my sister, this of course involves you because you will also stand to benefit from it as part of my family."

My mouth goes dry as I say in a whisper, "What's the deal?"

"Marriage, Sophia, the same as it always was."

I blink back the tears and say roughly, "No."

Tobias looks surprised. "Maybe you should hear the details before making a rash statement."

Lucian appears to be enjoying himself because he has the look of a hunter towering over the prey he just caught. He leans toward me and his breath fans the flames of anger as he whispers, "Nonna has decided she needs to see the next generation before she gets much older. She has instructed us all to provide her with it as a matter of urgency. That is why I am here, Sophia, to give her what she wants."

"How could you?"

I stand and face my brother with fire in my eyes. "How dare you sign my life away as part of a business deal? I thought you were better than that, Tobias, but obviously not.

Well, I won't do it, do you hear me? I will not agree to anything you say."

"Sophia."

A soft voice from behind me stops me in my tracks and I spin around as if I'm seeing a ghost.

"Maverick?" I whisper his name as if he will disappear like a mirage, but he doesn't. Instead, he moves toward me, looking so fierce it takes my breath away. As I take a step toward him, he does the same and soon I fall into those familiar strong arms that wrap around me and keep the whole world out.

He leans down and whispers, "I missed you."

I squeeze him harder and for a moment, it's just us, the two of us shutting the whole world away. Then he reluctantly pulls apart and taking my hand, turns to face the people patiently waiting, watching with interest.

CHAPTER 34

MAVERICK

When I saw Sophia, my whole world righted itself and I knew. I love her. The expression on her face told me she feels the same and as I held her in my arms, I knew I had made the right decision. Now I must set the wheels in motion and turn to face our respective brothers.

I hold out my hand to Tobias. "It's good to finally meet you, Mr. Moretti."

"Tobias, please." He shakes my hand and I see the curiosity in his eyes as he stares thoughtfully between us. Sophia is looking extremely worried and Lucian laughs. "Can somebody please put that poor girl out of her misery before she passes out?"

Sophia stares at him in surprise and Tobias growls, "Do you honestly think I was trading you as some kind of breeding mule?"

She looks surprised. "It certainly felt that way."

Tobias looks angry. "No, my business with Lucian concerned a different girl entirely."

Lucian nods and I see the smug look of victory in his eyes

as he turns to me and gloats. "Tobias had some information we were desperate for and used it to secure our future. We have formed an alliance where one family protects the other. We carry on with business as usual but if anything changes, we give first refusal to the other family. If we are challenged, we come together and face our enemies as one."

I look between them and say with interest. "Then the information he has must be very powerful."

Tobias nods. "It is."

He waves to the seats nearby and as we take them, I pull Sophia close to my side. She fits like a glove as I always knew she would and I hold her hand tightly so she can never escape me again. Tobias remains silent until we have each been served a drink and then, as the waiters head back inside, he says evenly, "When Carlos Toledo died, he had on him some powerful evidence."

Sophia stiffens beside me and I squeeze her hand reassuringly. "It was a memory stick that contained information on just about every family in the country. Their secrets and evidence that could blow their operations apart in the wrong hands. It was his intention to use this information to bargain for a place with the strongest family, ensuring his own protection. It didn't work."

Tobias's eyes glitter dangerously and Sophia shifts nervously in her seat as the tension swirls around us like a choking fog.

"I have evidence that the Romanos would kill to obtain and so, I have exchanged this in return for an alliance."

"So, this was all a lie, the grandchildren, the marriage, what was that all about?"

Sophia is angry and almost spits her words like venom and Lucian says darkly. "Nobody lied, Sophia. Nonna wants grandchildren more than anything right now and as it turns out, she already has one."

My head spins and I say in shock, "Ava?"

Lucian nods and for a moment we share a look that only we understand. Tobias was right, this is powerful information indeed.

Lucian carries on in a bitter voice. "He knows where Ava is hiding with Dante's son. Now we just have to go and fetch them."

From the look in his eye, that means trouble along the line and I wonder if Dante knows.

As if he heard my unspoken question, Lucian shakes his head and I wonder how my brother will react. As if it's his cue to leave, Lucian stands and says darkly, "I must go. I believe you have something for me."

Tobias nods and reaches inside his pocket and draws out a memory stick and hands it to my brother.

"The information is on here. I copied it from the one Carlos had on him, I hope it helps."

Lucian just nods and then turns to Ana and Sophia and bows. "Ladies, if you will excuse me, it has been a pleasure."

He shakes Tobias's hand and whispers something in his ear that makes Tobias nod and I see a smile pass between them that settles my heart. Yes, Lucian may be a bastard, but he's not stupid enough to look a gift horse in the mouth. He would be wise to keep Tobias close because his future is a deadly one. Then he turns to me and pulls me in for a hug, whispering, "Don't be a stranger, Lorenzo."

Then he leaves without a backward glance and I watch the usual circus close around him before they disappear into the darkness.

Tobias turns and smiles. "Maybe now is the time to settle our own family business."

He looks at Sophia with a gentle expression and I can tell he loves her a great deal. She is tense and must be wondering what's happening, and Tobias says in a gruff voice. "I called Maverick and asked him to meet us here for a reason."

"You called him?"

Sophia turns and looks at me in surprise and I nod. "As it happens, I was here anyway, waiting to beg you to come back with me."

"But…"

Sophia is speechless, which causes Tobias to laugh loudly. "That's something you don't see very often."

Ana nudges him and Tobias leans forward and takes his sister's hands. "Sophia, you are my sister and the only thing I want is your happiness. I can tell that Maverick makes you happy, but I am in agreement with his grandmother."

Sophia looks worried and he smiles sympathetically. "You have just met and yet are prepared to give everything up for love. I called Maverick to give my blessing for you to return with him to the Reapers and take it slowly and discover if this is really what you both want. You will always have a home with me, but it's time for you to spread your wings and fly. Maverick has also been set free to find himself and both families want this union to work because Maverick's grandmother sees your union as one of love and wants nothing more than for her grandson to be happy. If he is, she will be happy because she is hoping for a grandchild to care for sooner rather than later."

I roll my eyes as Sophia colors up and blushes prettily. Then she turns to me and says shyly, "Is this what you want?"

"You know it is." I pull her close and brush my lips against hers and whisper, "I'm taking you home, darlin'."

CHAPTER 35

SOPHIA

As soon as our business was concluded, Tobias and Ana retired to their cabin, leaving me and Maverick alone for the first time in what feels like a lifetime ago. As we sit wrapped in each other arms, on the deck of the Island Star, with the gentle lap of the waves as the only sound, I can't quite believe Maverick is here. It's like the most fabulous dream and I can't get close enough to him and it appears he feels the same way because he growls, "Never leave me again, Sophia, it hurts too much."

"Leave you? I never left willingly. Your grandmother arranged it, telling me that things had changed and you were giving it all up to live with the Reapers. She told me I had no place in that and was being sent back to my brother."

I still feel so hurt as the memory of rejection comes back for a visit and Maverick shakes his head angrily. "She had no right to interfere. She wanted to use you to bring me back to the family and when she saw it wouldn't work, decided to make my life as empty as possible, hoping I would give up and return home. I've only just learned that she even changed your number in my phone, which she subsequently had disconnected. She knew that if I had you beside me, I had everything I wanted in the world and I expect she was going to use you in the future to bring me home again."

"But why, surely she just wants your happiness?"

"You forget, Sophia, family is everything to the Romanos and they can't understand that a member of the family could be happy outside it. Their plan backfired when you said no and I threatened them. This was their Plan B and as it turned out, they got more than they bargained for. Dante's problem will keep them busy for a while, leaving us to see where we go from here."

"Where do you want that to be?"

I'm almost fearful to ask but have my answer when he kisses me deeply and says roughly, "I want it all, darlin'. Marriage. Babies, a little home set in the grounds of the Rubicon and the odd weekend with the Romanos to keep them sweet. I may have turned my back on my duty, but I will never turn my back on them. They are my blood and this way we get to enjoy all that is good about that, without any of the fucked-up fear that goes with it. We can have it all and exist outside of the darkness and live among honest people who have values that match our own. If you're up for it, darlin', I want to do all that with you as my old lady because if I've learned anything, it's that you are the perfect match for me."

He crushes my lips to his and there are no more words. It's actions that count now and it's time to show him.

We crash into the cabin that is luckily on the other side of the boat, far enough away from Tobias and Ana not to make an embarrassing conversion at breakfast.

As soon as we are inside the room, we tear off our clothes with a haste that makes us both laugh as we fall onto the bed and cling to each other as if we're imprisoned by invisible bonds.

Maverick is a wild man in every way and tonight is no exception. As he kisses me fiercely, I return it with a passion that surprises me. He tortures my body with kisses and gentle nips and drags his tongue all the way down my thighs, before parting my folds and biting and sucking my clit, causing me to stifle a scream that is threatening to push me over the edge before I'm ready. I shift closer to him and then he takes one of my legs and lifts it high in the air and growls, "I can't wait another minute."

Then he thrusts inside me with an ownership that causes my heart to twist in delicious pleasure as I feel him inside, rocking against me, filling and stretching me until there is nothing left to fill. I groan as I feel him own me, and gasp as he runs his hands over my ass and pulls me harder against him. I grip his balls in a strong, unforgiving grip, reminding him that he's mine. He grunts and moans my name over and over again and then pulls out as suddenly as he went in, before reaching for a condom from his jeans and tearing it open with his teeth.

Then he growls, "We're going to have to either protect you, or book the preacher because I want to fill you completely with everything I have."

I smile with an understanding that neither of us are going anywhere anytime soon and this is going to be on repeat for the foreseeable future. It's as if he chases the last shadow away as my heart fills so full with happiness, I feel as if I've been reborn. I'm no longer that frightened controlled princess who fears the world. I own it now because I am free. Released into the unknown with a magnificent warrior by my side. We will be ok. Of that, I am certain.

For the next two weeks, we make the most of every minute we have on the Island Star. Maverick settles into the family as if he has always been there. He forges a strong bond with Tobias and they have much in common. Ana adores him and we enjoy a leisurely vacation with the family we always will be. I never imagined love would feel like this. We have it all and I never thought I'd say that.

So, it's with regret that we reach our final destination because Tobias and Ana will be continuing their travels in Europe and we are returning to start our life at the Rubicon.

It's hard to say goodbye to my brother and my much-loved sister-in-law but we do so with the promise of meeting up soon and then head off alone without the usual guards and black cars. Instead, we take a cab to the airport and join the rest of civilization aboard a commercial jet bound for Washington.

CHAPTER 36

MAVERICK

I can see her in the distance and it strikes me just how well I've trained her the past six months. Where it used to be easy to hunt her down, she is now making it increasingly difficult to do. I can tell which way she's heading though and still have a few tricks left up my sleeve, although that's a joke because as usual, I'm not wearing any.

Ducking to the side, I make to head her off via a shortcut I know well and hope she ends up where I want her to be. If she goes off track, everything will be ruined.

I suppose I make it with just a couple of minutes to spare and take a moment to catch my breath because I will need to keep my feelings in check.

Hearing the twigs from the forest crunch under her feet, I set my mood accordingly and lie low where I know she will pass. As she moves closer, I reach my hand out and spin her against me as she passes and place my other hand over her eyes.

"Gotcha."

She struggles, but it's futile because we both know she ain't going anywhere.

I pull her hard against me and growl, "Make it easy on yourself, darlin', if you do, this will be a whole lot easier."

"For who?"

Her voice is husky and laced with desire and I'm guessing if I ripped off those tiny shorts she wears, she would be wet and ready. I almost deviate from the plan as I feel her trembling body against mine and feel the desire wafting through the trees in the early morning air. Then again, morning has a long way to come because night is still ruling this particular hour and as I lead her to where I need her most, I feel my heart thumping with a nervousness that has no reason being here.

She whimpers as I gently bite her neck like the hungriest of vampires and she pushes back against my chest, wriggling against my cock. It's almost unbearable as I fight my own battle within myself not to swing her against the trunk of the nearest tree and claim my woman like the savage beast I am.

I whisper huskily in her ear, "Stop struggling and open your eyes."

Whipping my hand away, I hear her gasp as she sees what's waiting and spins to face me with an expression that brings out the emotion in a man that never knew he had any.

"It's beautiful."

She turns and looks in wonder at the magical fantasy I have created just for her as she sees the forest transformed into a fairy tale.

Candles burn in little glass jars set around a bed made from the fruits of the forest. Branches, twigs and moss have formed the base of a bed strewn with leaves and finished off with a huge soft blanket that will provide comfort—for a while at least. As the candle flames dance in the light of the disappearing darkness, she turns to me and her eyes are bright as she whispers, "I love you, Maverick."

Pulling her face to mine with two hands cupped either side of her beauty, I take my fill of the lips I will never tire of tasting.

I'm not rough, I take it gentle and slow and savor the moment because this one is a long time coming.

Running my hands under her top, I ease it from her back and marvel at the beauty nature created.

Leaning down, I kiss her soft skin, bathed in a sheen of sweat and relish the taste of a woman in her prime. She gasps and it sends the heat tearing through my body as I physically ache to make her mine in every way possible.

I move my mouth down her body, inhaling the toxic fumes of lust and as I reach her shorts, I use my teeth to tear them from her like the frantic beast I am. On my instructions she wears nothing else and as I taste her arousal; it makes my cock throb so hard it could all be over in seconds.

She pushes into me trying to bring us closer but not yet.

Standing, I swing her into my arms and carry her to the bed I made especially for her and lay her gently on the blanket. My own shorts follow hers to a heap on the ground and as I position myself above my beautiful lady, I whisper, "I love you, Sophia."

The tears roll down her face and the light in her eyes causes my heart to burst as she whispers back, "Not as much as I love you, Maverick."

Pulling her toward me, I push inside and move slowly and gently, relishing the ease in which her body welcomes me in. She molds herself around me once again, reinforcing the fact that we were made for each other. Gently, slowly, I fill my woman with everything I've got and as she moans my name, I catch the words in my mouth that can't ever get enough of the woman beneath me.

Unlike our usual lovemaking, this one is less frantic, less brutal and has all the makings of a love story because this is *our* love story, the tale of when two lost souls found each other in the most terrifying of ways and conquered it all to live happily ever after. As Sophia clenches my cock and shatters around me, I cum so hard it causes the birds to wake up screeching from the trees. As she throbs and pulses beneath me as I hold her tenderly, I say in the softest voice I have ever used, "Will you marry me, Sophia Moretti?"

She stills and I feel her tears wet against my cheek as she clings to me hard and kisses me lightly across my face. Then she looks at me with the purest look of love there is and says shyly, "No."

For a moment we cling together and savor the moment that was always going to happen since we met. I think back to the struggle that brought us to this point and stroke her hair and kiss her lovingly, before gently setting her down on the blanket. As I pull out and roll on my back, I pull her face to my chest and twist her hair in my hands, pulling it gently to punish her for being so brutal.

She sighs against my skin and it makes me smile because no one was more surprised than me to discover that Sophia likes to feel the bite of pain more than she likes it gentle.

She snuggles into me and says dreamily, "Thank you, Maverick, that was perfect."

"Get used to it, darlin' because you're going nowhere, despite turning me down."

We share a laugh and just savor the moment because as moments go, this one's for the history books.

CHAPTER 37

SOPHIA

I have never been so happy. I never thought I would be, but these last six months have been the happiest of my life. When we returned to the Rubicon, it was to the party that Ashton promised me. It felt so good to return with Maverick by my side and it didn't take long for us to settle into our life here as a couple. I soon learned that my fear was unfounded because nothing scares me now. I help with the kids during the day and in the bar at night, under the watchful eye of the man who lights the flame to my soul. I love chatting to the other women and spending time with them, which I discovered is extremely welcome when dealing with the men that live here. Rough, crude and so hot, we need no heating because life at the Rubicon is, as Millie said, the stuff of dreams.

Millie herself has become a firm friend of mine and never once made me feel awkward. I am beginning to realize just how special these girls are because there is not a bad bone in any of them and never having the friendship of women before; I guard ours fiercely and protect it like the precious thing it is.

The sun finally breaks through the drapes in the bedroom I share with Maverick. I never thought I would be so happy but I am. He completes me and as the man himself enters the room; I have to laugh because the sight of him brings the biggest smile to my lips.

"Morning, darlin' - finally."

He winks because as soon as we returned from the forest, he started all over again and I fell into a deep sleep fueled by exhaustion. However, I am immediately awake as he enters the room with nothing but a tray covering him, laden with pancakes and juice with a side of fruit. He is buck naked and my mouth waters as I see the beast who captured my heart in all his magnificent glory. His hair is long and wild and his muscles flex as he sets the tray on the side table, giving me a delicious view of his ass. My mouth waters for more than the food he has served me so cheekily and the bed sags as he sits beside me and pulls me up to face him. Running his hand around my head, he holds me firmly and looks into my eyes and his eyes glint with a resolve I know only too well.

Then he almost growls, "Sophia Moretti, I am a patient man but have now reached the end of it. I am not accustomed to asking the same question, what will now be three times, and I expect the right answer this time. From the minute we first met, you have been difficult, arrogant and tested my patience. You have done your best to make my life as difficult as possible and I have crossed Oceans to bring you back to me. I gave up my family for you and turned my back on a life that would make me want for nothing but one thing."

He seems almost emotional as he rests his head against mine and says softly, "You. I gave all that up for you because you are worth more to me than life itself. I couldn't begin to live a life without you in it because you are the breath in my lungs and the blood in my veins. You give me strength and purpose and you own my heart and soul. So, will you fucking marry me, you annoying woman and put me out of my misery once and for all?"

"Yes."

My voice is but a whisper and the tears that fall are the happiest I have ever shed.

"Yes, I will marry you. It was always going to be a yes, you know that because who else would ever put up with you?"

I smile through my tears as his eyes light up and the happiness shines through the darkness. The emotion in the room is palpable and as he traces the lines of my face, he whispers huskily, "I love you, Sophia Moretti but I am in love forever with Sophia Romano."

Our lips meet in a kiss that relegates the breakfast to the trash. I no longer need food when I have everything I want holding me so tenderly in his arms. As he lowers me to the bed, I plan on showing him just how much he means to me because I intend on feasting on a different banquet this morning and what a tasty one it is.

EPILOGUE

MILLIE

My head hurts, I think I've lost the power of taste and I feel sore and bruised from a night that hasn't ended yet. As party's go, this one was the mother of them all and it makes me so happy we could give Sophia and Maverick the send-off they deserved.

If I feel a tinge of regret, it doesn't last long because I quickly laid that particular infatuation to rest. Maverick may have been the sexiest man I have ever met but seeing him with Sophia, told me it means nothing when they don't feel the same. Watching them this past few months has taught me a lot. She has brought him out of his shell in a way I never could and it annoys me to hell and back that I love her like the sister I never had. When Angel left, I was cut adrift in an empty boat of my own making. I have learned to embrace change since living here and roll with the punches because life is never dull for a second.

It wasn't hard to pick up the fragile pieces of my heart and glue them back together because the guys here make it impossible to stay lonely for long.

However, the party last night was not just to celebrate the

happy couple's approaching wedding, it was to celebrate my own exit from a life I never thought I'd walk away from.

"Hey, Millie, you should get some sleep, don't you have a long day ahead of you tomorrow?"

I look up and see Bonnie wandering through the bar, bleary-eyed, as she looks around with disgust at the mess left behind.

"Oh, you know, old habits and all, I thought I'd leave this place as I'd want to find it before packing my bags."

She looks a little concerned. "Will you be ok?"

"I hope so." I feel slightly nervous and she smiles with a genuine warmth that always makes her one of the most approachable women here.

Grabbing a stool, she pulls me down beside her and takes my hand, looking deep into my eyes. "You know, you can back out, it's not for long; this is still your home."

"I know that and it's fine." I smile with a bravery I'm not sure is real because I have lived here for close on two years and life is easy. However, it became apparent when Angel left and Maverick found happiness with Sophia, that I wanted more. So, Ryder arranged a little mission of my own and I am excited to see it through.

Bonnie says with interest. "Are you all set?"

I nod with an excitement that has been growing since he first asked me. "To be honest, Bonnie, I am so ready for this. I need this more than anything and if it goes well, I can return here and feel as if I really earned my place."

Bonnie laughs and shakes her head. "I think you can safely say you earned your place here, honey."

She winks and I laugh. "It's not hard. This place is paradise for a single girl who has no shame. No, this time it's different because I'm out on my own. It should help me discover the direction I'm heading and I'm impatient for that."

Bonnie nods and says thoughtfully, "You know, it's not dissimilar to how I came here. When Snake found me, I was doing the very thing you are expected to do."

"Any pointers?" I smile but it's edged with tension because this is serious and I know a lot's at stake.

"It was fine, you have trained well for it, after all, you have run this bar like a pro."

We laugh because she's right there and she gets a faraway look in her eyes as she smiles softly. "I never knew it would end up here though. When Snake kidnapped me and virtually held me prisoner, I thought my life had ended. Little did I know he was saving me in the process. You know, I wouldn't change a thing about what happened and I hope to God you find happiness for yourself because there is nothing like the excitement of danger that fires a woman's soul."

I feel a shiver of excitement as I think about the task Ryder set me. The Dragon's Ruin. It sounds exciting, let alone the reason I'm there. I wonder where it will end, right back here, I hope.

As if she reads my mind, Bonnie says firmly, "You know, one word will bring the cavalry calling, don't you?"

I nod. "Of course, I will always have the guy's protection, that goes without saying. The thing is, Bonnie, living among the Reapers has taught me that great rewards come with a little risk involved. I watch those men ride out of here to save the world and when they come back, I am only too happy to give them comfort to chase the bad memories away. The thing is, I want to taste a little danger for myself and the Dragon's Ruin sounds just the place to find it."

Bonnie nods and then smiles sweetly. "Let me help you clean this place up. Two pairs of hands are better than one and you can tell me all about it as we work."

"Don't you have to get back to Snake?"

She shakes her head. "No, he's deep in conversation with

Ryder. They're putting the final touches to your mission and setting the protection in place you need."

As we set to work, Bonnie tells me about her own experience in a world I am to inhabit until the job is done. It doesn't sound as glamorous as it is here and serves the purpose not to dress this up in excitement because I'm in no doubt this is a special place and there is none to equal it. However, The Dragon's Ruin sounds like my kind of place and I am itching to see what that involves. Will I be back, you bet because as homes go, this is one you never want to move out of. I just hope that I bring back a whole lot of memories to keep me warm at night because it's about time Millie made her mark.

Carry on reading Millie's story in
Catch a King

To save a King, you need to slay a dragon.

Millie

I have one job. Go undercover at the Dragon's Ruin, MC Club and find out why one of them is asking questions about the president of The Twisted Reapers MC, Ryder King.
I will not let them down.
They are my family, my protectors, my lovers.
To be a Reaper, you have to think and act like one, and the bikers at the Dragon's Ruin are going to discover that the hard way.
Until him.
Sawyer. A bandeau wearing hot mess of darkness.
Violent obsidian eyes, full of lust and promising to wrap me in shadows.
So dangerous he will be the ruin of me and threaten to smash my principles into jagged edges of betrayal.
When he turns his attention to me, I'm suddenly not so brave.
Will I betray my own family for one second with him, or will he ultimately use me to bring the Twisted Reapers down?
There are five kings. At the end of this, will there be four?

Five kings is the explosive new series by Stella Andrews. Catch a King is the first and kick starts a trail through the darkness to find the Ruler of them all. Five powerful men who belong to an exclusive club where membership requires you to leave your soul at the door. Someone is out to bring them down, and each book tells their story and the women that break them.
If you like your books on the darker side, this series may be for you. Hot, dark and twisted with romance running like a river of pleasure through its pages.
Each book can be read standalone and there NO cliffhangers.

If you enjoyed Broken Beauty, please would you be so kind as to leave a review on Amazon?

Join my closed Facebook Group

Stella's Sexy Readers

Follow me on Instagram

Stay healthy and happy and thanks for reading xx

Carry on reading for more Reaper Romances, Mafia Romance & more.
stellaandrews.com.

MORE BOOKS

Twisted Reapers

Sealed With a Broken Kiss
Dirty Hero (Snake & Bonnie)
Daddy's Girls (Ryder & Ashton)
Twisted (Sam & Kitty)
The Billion Dollar baby (Tyler & Sydney)
Bodyguard (Jet & Lucy)
Flash (Flash & Jennifer)
Country Girl (Tyson & Sunny)

The Romanos
The Throne of Pain (Lucian & Riley)
The Throne of Hate (Dante & Isabella)
The Throne of Fear (Romeo & Ivy)
Lorenzo's story is in Broken Beauty

Beauty Series
Breaking Beauty (Sebastian & Angel) *
Owning Beauty (Tobias & Anastasia)
Broken Beauty (Maverick & Sophia) *
Completing Beauty – The series

Five Kings
Catch a King (Sawyer & Millie) *
Slade

Steal a King

Break a King

Destroy a King

Marry a King

Baron

Club Mafia

Club Mafia – The Contract

Club Mafia – The Boss

Club Mafia – The Angel

Club Mafia – The Savage

Standalone

The Highest Bidder (Logan & Samantha)

Rocked (Jax & Emily)

Brutally British

Deck the Boss

Reasons to sign up to my mailing list.

- A reminder that you can read my books FREE with Kindle Unlimited.
- Receive a monthly newsletter so you don't miss out on any special offers or new releases.
- Links to follow me on Amazon or social media to be kept up to date with new releases.
- Free books and bonus content.
- Opportunities to read my books before they are even released by joining my team.
- Sneak peeks at new material before anyone else.

stellaandrews.com

Printed in Great Britain
by Amazon